I0545273

Axed at the Ice Machine

A Mattie Tucker Paranormal Cozy Mystery, Volume 1

Juliette Harper

Published by Gray Cat Publishing, 2022.

AXED AT THE ICE MACHINE

First edition. March 4, 2022.

Copyright © 2022 Juliette Harper.

ISBN: 978-1943516100

Written by Juliette Harper.

Chapter 1

In Miller's Cove, we pride ourselves on being the most out-of-step town in the south. Every business on our Main Street, which has been used for multiple movies set in the 1940s and 1950s, offers some service most people don't believe the modern world needs.

We made the transformation on purpose. Hank Leonard, the town mayor, read about a place in Georgia that reinvented itself as an Alpine ski village. In Georgia!

If they can get tourists to come spend money pretending they're in Switzerland or some such place, Hank decided the people of Miller's Cove could put ourselves on the map in Tennessee.

Go to any bookstore and ask the clerk to show you books about time travel. You'll be reading for a year. Miller's Cove will take you to World War II on a Friday and send you right back to the 21st century when you start the drive home Sunday night.

Heaven knows the town was drying up and dying until we adopted anachronism as our theme. Personally, I think Hank sold the idea when he used that word—theme.

Most of the local women understood that term at a cellular level. Pageant aspirations are as contagious as the measles in this neck of the woods. I have the distinction of being the only woman in my high school graduating class who never competed for a tiara of any kind.

Something told me being Miss Tennessee Tractor and Plow wouldn't look good on a modern woman's resume. Little did I know that wasn't going to be a problem in my life.

At the time, no one thought much about my lack of Southern runway pride. They just clucked their tongues and said, "Well, she's a Tucker. What do you expect?"

Maybelle Antoinette Tucker, to be exact. Maybelle after Mother Maybelle Carter, God rest her guitar-scratching heart, and Antoinette after that queen who told people to eat cake instead of bread. I'm iffy on the middle name, by the way, since things didn't work out well for her and her husband.

Thankfully, people have been calling me Mattie since my feet first touched the ground. It's the initials—MAT—Mattie. My situation isn't unique. Everyone in town has a nickname.

Mayor Leonard goes by Buckshot on account of an accident involving an outhouse that he doesn't like to discuss. The idea to become the most out-of-step community in the state, however, really goes to Skeet Abbott's wife Alma who loves Rudolph the Red-Nosed Reindeer.

As soon as Buckshot said the town needed a theme, Alma stood up in the city council meeting and declared, "In Rudolph, everything that couldn't be fixed got sent to the Island of Misfit Toys. The whole story got worked out right there, so why can't we be misfits?"

Here's the truth. We already were misfits. My people, the Tuckers, are witches. Buckshot Leonard, like his daddy before him, gets a little furry when the moon is full. And don't try lying to Alma Abbott because she's a truth demon.

But even a little town filled with magical and paranormal creatures has to make a living. Even the ghosts at the cemetery agreed to that. Our natural-born skills aren't the kind of things we let outsiders know about. Our theme needed to be more socially acceptable and Alma, with her unerring intuition, hit the bull's eye with her first shot.

Everyone in the room started buzzing, talking about their old-fashioned hobbies or things their ancestors did to make a living. My Daddy kicked off the practical action saying he'd open up an horology shop. The ladies from the Baptist Church about had a fit until Daddy straightened them out on the definition of horology, which has to do with keeping time not charging for it.

Daddy, God rest his soul, was a time witch. He could bring any broken timepiece back to life with a combination of skilled hands and enchantment. Thank God my Uncle Grimshaw—Grim for short—has the same talent, because even if I am an horologist's daughter, I'm always late and I can't wear a watch. Not even a digital one. Strap a watch on my wrist and it's dead before you get the band buckled.

Don't judge. I have issues with my body's electromagnetic field. I should kill smartphones and computers—really anything technological—but I don't. Thank Hecate for that, because in addition to murdering clocks, my wonky EMF draws in every unhappy ghost in a 500-square mile radius.

Technically, I do run the clock shop with Uncle Grim since Daddy passed, but I have to cast a barrier spell on myself before I can even walk in the door. I forgot one time last year right before the big weekend-before-Christmas sale and Uncle Grim still hasn't let me hear the last of it.

The day this story begins, I pulled up behind the store in my vintage 1948 Dodge. That's right. Since the tourists started coming to Miller's Cove, we've embraced the anachronistic vibe. I drive a baby blue deluxe D24 sedan. She's half a block of sinuous curves with immaculate white walls and running boards.

When I parked beside Grim's Model A and got out to douse myself in barrier magic, a polite cough from the wisteria bushes on the other side of the alley made me jump half out of my skin. Turning, I confronted the ghost of a man dressed in modern clothing, so, not a local.

At the time I was wearing a gorgeous pair of navy wide-legged pleated trousers I could have stolen right out of Katherine Hepburn's closet and a white blouse with a swoopy "M" over the left shoulder.

With my long, honey brown hair done up in a thick roll at the back of my neck, I was absolutely ready for my close up, Mr. DeMille. Taking off my vintage sunglasses, I addressed the spirit. "Good morning. Can I help you?"

"Geez lady, just the fact that you can see me and talk to me helps. I'm dead, aren't I?"

"Yes, sir. It would appear so. What happened?"

"My wife and I are staying at the Nostalgia Nook Lodge out on the highway. The one that looks like it belongs in a movie."

That could describe every building in town, but I didn't say so. "I know the place."

"Well, I went to get ice and somebody knocked me in the head. See?"

With that, he turned around and showed me the hatchet sticking out of the back of his head. At least I wasn't going to have to worry about cause of death.

"I do see that," I agreed. "Listen, mister...

"It's Frank."

"Listen, Frank. You've already got a leg up on most folks in your situation. You know you're dead, so you can move on along to the next level. You'll either see a light or somebody from the other side will come to get you. Just be patient."

He looked at me like I was the one with a blade in the cranium. "Lady, I'm not going anywhere. If somebody did this to me, my wife is next. You've got to help her."

I'd like to tell you all that my days don't usually start off like that, but why begin a new friendship with a lie? The sign out front say's Tucker's Horology, but I'm a paranormal private investigator, and I just got a new client. Hopefully I'd be able to keep the wife and her checkbook alive long enough to get paid.

Chapter 2

A BLAST OF GLENN MILLER hit me full in the face when I opened the back door. Our local radio station switched over to antiquated vacuum tubes last year. Visitors can't get over the rich, resonance the equipment brings to Big Band.

Grim stopped whistling *String of Pearls* long enough to say, "You're late." He didn't bother to look up from the pocket watch mounted in clamps on his workbench. With his magnifying loupes lowered over his gold spectacles, my uncle looked like an extra on a Steampunk movie.

"Five minutes," I groused, "and I would have made it if Frank here hadn't stopped me to talk."

That made Grim look up. Flipping the magnifiers up over his eyebrows, he took a good look at the ghost who hovered uncertainly just inside the door.

"Dang son, that must have hurt."

Frank made a tentative move to touch the hatchet. "I don't really remember. What's that ticking?"

Grim made a clucking sound. "Blade went deep, didn't it? This is a clock shop."

Frank blinked, clearly not following the explanation.

Making a second attempt Grim said, "Clocks tick. This is a *clock* shop."

Finally catching on, Frank said, "I use my iPhone for a clock. My grandmother had a clock that ticked. I don't know how anybody could sleep with one of those things on the bedside table."

"That's how I feel about one of those dinging, burping gizmos," Grim grumbled.

5

My uncle, like many citizens of Miller's Cove, has zero problem living in the past. Turning his attention back to me, Grim said, "I guess this means you're not working in the shop today."

"We have to take a ride out to the Nostalgia Nook and check on Frank's wife. He's worried she's in danger. Sorry."

Grim gave me a mischievous smile. "I'm sure Press will be thrilled to see you pull up after last time."

I winced. Our local chief of police, Preston Jackson, doesn't like to work cases in daylight. He floats a story about anemia-related light sensitivity to the tourists, but you put tooth and tooth together with that guy and you come up with fang.

My last case involved a sunburnt ghost and a singed corpse. When the killer startled me, I put out a burst of EMF that flipped the switch on a tanning bed.

First off, the Reminiscent Riviera Spa shouldn't have that kind of equipment on site. It's not period correct. Tanning beds weren't invented until 1978. Second, how was I supposed to know a vampire can suffer third-degree burns from high-tech light bulbs?

Here's the deal with me and Preston. He's read too many Sam Spade novels. Seen too many Humphrey Bogart movies. Which fits, because he was turned in Chicago in the Thirties.

Press doesn't have to shop for those pinstripe, double-breasted suits and wingtips. He just had to take them out of storage when the town went retro. Same for his shoulder holster and pistol.

You'd think the two of us would be a perfect fit since every time I get near the man, I have Lauren Bacall fantasies. I can see myself leaning against a door frame and husking, "You know how to whistle, don't you, Press? You just put your lips together and blow."

Which would be great if I didn't annoy and/or try to get him permanently dead on a regular basis. If I knew my vamp, he was out at the Nostalgia Nook right now selling the murder as part of the town's "act" to prevent panic among the civilians.

"Frank's death involves an ice machine," I assured Grim. "There's no way to harm a vampire with ice, right?"

Flipping his magnifiers back in place, my uncle gave me a bug-eyed shrug. "Not that I know of, but if there is, I'm sure you'll find it."

I sarcastically thanked Grim for the vote of confidence and motioned to Frank to turn around and go back outside. When I climbed in the driver's seat of the Dodge, the ghost looked momentarily confused.

"Just step through the door," I instructed. "You'll be fine."

One foot came through the door just under the handle. "Hey! This is pretty cool," he said, sliding the rest of the way into the car. "If I can pass through the door, why don't I fall through the seat?"

"Good question," I said, starting the Dodge and putting the big beauty in reverse. "You're new to being a spirit. Didn't you ever see that movie *Ghost*?"

He frowned. "Something about a potter's wheel?"

"Close enough," I said, looking over my shoulder and twisting the steering wheel at the same time to avoid the wisteria. "You haven't been dead long enough to figure out how to pick things up or manipulate objects, but the remaining essence of your body remembers how to sit down. You'll get better at doing things the longer you're dead."

That got me a laugh. "That's funny. Death doesn't seem like an improvable condition."

The humor was a good sign. Sometimes I get ghosts who don't want to do anything but talk about how they can't possibly be dead, completely ignoring things like gaping gunshot wounds to the chest or gruesome head injuries like Frank's.

With the nose of the Dodge now headed straight down the alley toward Main Street, I said, "Not to be indelicate, Frank, but we need to talk business. I don't help people like you out of the goodness of my heart."

Technically, that wasn't a true statement. The bulk of my cases are pro bono work, a fancy term for "freebie." But I do at least make an effort to get the ghost's living relatives to pay me, which is what I explained to Frank.

To my astonishment, the guy had the nerve to ask, "What special skills do you bring to the job?"

If we hadn't been on Main Street, I would have slammed on the brakes and told the ingrate to get out of my car. "You mean other than being able to see you? That's not special enough for you?"

"Well," he admitted, "that is a big help, but are you any good at solving crimes?"

At this juncture in my undead relationships, I normally take the time to explain that I am a witch with a specific skill set. The Tuckers are hereditary solitary practitioners. Our magic is unique to the family and manifests differently in each of us.

If we're splitting hairs, I self-identify as a solitary hereditary eclectic hedge witch. I'm great at every day practical magic, but I can whip up a potion in a pinch. My late mother was a sigil/word witch. I inherited her ability to decipher signs and signals—what some people call clues.

Daddy's time magic hit my system in the womb and created what my kin refer to as "Mattie's problem," since they're nice enough not to use the phrase "birth defect." However, without my dysfunctional electromagnetic field, I wouldn't draw in clients, so the genetics balance out in the end.

Since Frank had shifted our conversation into a job interview, I gave him the short version, "I'm a witch with enough power to solve your problem or see to it you're stuck like this forever."

Even though ghosts have no need to swallow his Adam's apple bobbed in a convulsive gulp. "You're hired. I'll make sure Vanessa pays you."

By this time we'd passed the city limits and were within a mile of The Nostalgia Nook. "Vanessa is your wife?"

"Yes. She must be so upset about this. The poor woman can't stand the sight of blood."

Cutting my eyes at him out of the corner of my sunglasses I said, "You think she's more upset about the blood than you being dead?"

"Oh," he said with bright cheerfulness, "she'll be sad for awhile, but I'm her fifth husband. She'll find somebody new before long."

As I slowed and flipped on the blinker to turn into the lodge's parking lot, I started to ask why they'd decided to vacation in Miller's Cove. That's when I spotted Preston Jackson. He stood under the shade of the canopy covering the lodge's main entrance, arms crossed over his chest.

With his superior vampire vision Press had likely spotted my baby blue behemoth a mile back on the highway. I couldn't see his eyes behind his own dark shades, but I didn't need the extra confirmation to know the vamp was glaring daggers in my direction.

With a dead tourist on his hands and cloudless, sunshiny weather, Preston Jackson's day was already ruined. My arrival on the scene was nothing but the big insulting cherry on top of the cake.

Chapter 3

———●———

PLASTERING WHAT I HOPED was a disarming smile on my face, I pulled under the covered drive and rolled down the window. A blast of warm air hit me in the face.

Believe it or not, cars have been air conditioned since 1940. I've boosted my original AC with magic. Don't buy what you see in the movies. Maintaining a vintage hairdo takes work. Heat and humidity are not your friends.

In keeping with my signature style, the first words out of my mouth were a mistake. "Hi, Press. Gorgeous day."

Vampires don't sweat, but Press had loosened his tie anyway, probably out of habit. The pink outlines of his healing third-degree burns stood out against his pale skin.

"Any day when the sun is up isn't gorgeous, Mattie. What are you doing here?"

Jerking my head toward the passenger seat, I said, "Your murder victim hired me to look after his wife."

Press leaned down and studied the car's interior. His proximity sent a thrill through me. He's a big man. Broad shouldered. Well built. Dark wavy hair contained with pomade. Still wearing the same cologne he used in 1935 when he had a pulse. Aqua Velva Ice Blue.

Clean. Masculine. Menthol, but my witch's nose picked up on lavender and vanilla with something like moss and oak underneath. What can I say? I do have a pulse. The undead detective looked good *and* smelled good.

My sensory fantasy lasted just long enough for Press to scan the other side of the front seat and bark, "What are you playing at, Mattie? There's nobody else in there."

I looked over at Frank who raised one hand and wiggled his fingers in my direction. "I haven't moved a muscle," the ghost assured me.

"You don't have muscles, Frank."

That got Press's attention. "Frank? Frank Reynolds?"

"Yeah," my client said, "that's me. Or I guess that *was* me. But I'm still me, so…"

Interrupting the babble, I turned back to Press. "He says that's his name."

What Press said next cost him, but he's a cop first and an annoyed wannabe boyfriend second. "He's the vic, all right. What's with this joker? Usually I see spooks just fine."

That was all the opening I needed to worm my way into his investigation. "I don't know, but if you'll let me park and give me a few, I'll find out."

The Nostalgia Nook has a policy. Modern cars go in the underground garage out of sight. Vintage rides like mine are welcome in the parking lot up top to add to the upscale log cabin lodge ambiance of the place.

"Fine," Press said. "The crime scene is on the west side. Park where I can see you and no snooping on your own."

He stepped away from the window. I put the car in drive and chose an empty spot beside a 1956 Red Cadillac woodie station wagon.

I started to speak to Frank, but the ghost's gaze was locked on something straight out the windshield. Following his line of sight, I saw the crime scene.

Local coroner, Santos Simpson, stood beside Frank's mortal remains—or at least the backside of them, which currently protruded out of the ice machine.

Santos appeared to be trying to figure out how to extract the corpse without destroying evidence. The practicing witch doctor who prefers the term "shaman," spotted me and waved.

The motion strained his white shirt enough for me to make out the outline of the protection necklace tucked under the cloth. He keeps the juju hidden out of deference to the tourists who might get upset at the sight of a circle of animal teeth around a guy's neck.

The other man on the scene, Press's partner, Jerry Michaels, glanced in my direction as well. He was using an old single lens reflex Rollei outfitted with a massive silver flash attachment to take crime scene photos.

I waved to both men. Press might not be happy to see me, but I'm on good terms with Santos, Jerry, and the two uniformed officers who were working crowd control—the O'Malley twins. Nicest couple of elves you'd ever want to meet.

Taking off my shades, I twisted in the seat and started to confront Frank, who was still staring out the window. "Why are you hiding from the cops?"

"I'm not doing it on purpose."

That I believed. Early in my PI career I learned that deception survives death. Whatever Frank had to hide now was probably the same thing that got him killed.

Gesturing toward the ice machine, I said, "Look at yourself, Frank. What do you see?"

"That I should have done those extra squats like my personal trainer wanted."

This was going to be a long day.

"Frank, you don't have to put half your body in the machine to get ice. What were you doing?"

An uncertain look came over his face. "I think I dropped something important inside. When I reached in to get it, someone hit me in the head. The next thing I knew, I was standing in an alley talking to you."

"What did you drop?"

"I don't remember."

"Okay, we're going to walk over there. Keep your mouth shut while I talk to the police unless you remember something important. Me talking to thin air won't look good for the tourists, got it?"

Finally turning toward me, the spirit's features melted into pure petulance. "Are you always this pushy?"

"No, usually I'm worse."

Even though I hadn't met his missus yet, I felt certain she wore the pants in the family. Frank wasn't necessarily a bad looking man absent the ax in the back of his head. His features reminded me of an art school project that didn't come out quite right.

A bulbous nose overpowered the weak chin, but he had a good jawline. All ghosts appear to me in washed out tones, but Frank would have been nondescript in living color.

So far I'd seen him swing from superior jerk over the question of my pay to whining brat complaining about me being pushy. In any murder, the spouse always tops the suspect list, but I could totally see Vanessa putting Frank out of *her* misery so she could move on to husband number six.

When the ghost floated out of the car, I eyed him in relation to the roof of the station wagon. I guessed that in life the man had stood around 5'7", an estimate confirmed when we joined Press and the team. The vampire tops out at an impressive 6'6". The ghost barely came up to his shoulder.

Short guy bending over an ice machine. Blow from above and behind. The killer could have been a man or a woman.

In deference to Press's sun aversion, we were standing under the overhang sheltering the ice machine and its companion, a vintage Coca-Cola chest filled with short, pale green bottles.

I eyed the curious crowd and their clicking cell phones. Hiding my words behind a fake smile, I said, "Is that a good idea?"

Press used the motions of lighting a cigarette to obscure his response. The man's dead already. Cigarettes won't kill him a second time, but I turned my back to the onlookers to put myself upwind from the second-hand smoke.

Shaking a Lucky out of the pack, Press clicked open a silver lighter. As he held the cigarette to the flame he said, "The social media screen will catch the posts. We'll make sure everybody gets a good dose of memory revision magic on their way over the county line."

Taking my phone out of the pocket of my slacks, I began to snap my own set of photos. I disguise the device inside a leather wallet and use a remote control built into a lipstick tube to activate the shutter.

Anyone taking in the scene would see a handsome man smoking a Lucky while the woman beside him touched up her make-up.

I knew what I was doing. Press couldn't object without giving the tourists an even better show. Instead he expelled a cloud of smoke and muttered, "Stop it."

Still snapping away, I said, "Don't be cranky, Press. I'm the only one who can talk to your victim, remember?"

"Is the stiff with you?"

Glancing over, I saw Frank watching Santos and Jerry work the scene. "Yeah. He's over there worried about how his butt looks sticking out of that ice machine."

Even though he couldn't have taken more than three drags, Press stubbed out his smoke in a nearby can of sand. "Round him up. I'm going to talk to the wife. Watch his reactions and tell me everything you see."

Affecting a wounded look, I said, "Press, I would never hold out on you."

For a microsecond I thought the corner of his mouth might curve into a smile, but he aborted the traitorous expression in its tracks. "Yeah. I've heard that one before. "

As the big galoot stomped off, I covered my mouth with my hand and coughed, "Come on, Frank."

The spirit drifted over. He looked like a dog who had just dodged a kick. "What are you so cheerful about?" he demanded, his voice breaking. "You could have some respect for the dead."

Whatever. Preston Jackson wanted me to come with him on an interview! I know. He only needed me to communicate with the vic's ghost, but the invitation was the first opening the vamp had given me since the tanning bed incident.

Maybe the ice in that machine wasn't the only thing thawing in Miller's Cove that morning.

Chapter 4

FRANK TOOK A LONG WALK to his demise. The Reynolds had been assigned a spectacular corner room with windows looking toward the mountains. A third uniformed officer, Patrick "Punk" Jones stood stolidly in front of the door when we approached.

"Hey, Punk, how's your mama and them?" I asked.

"Hey, Mattie. They're good. We're gonna be playing Saturday night. Come on over."

The Joneses are a clan of fairies. Punk hides a spectacular pair of iridescent wings under his blue uniform shirt. Music runs in their blood. They and their kind are some of the best pickers in these parts.

"I might just round up Uncle Grim and take you up on that."

"Tuckers are always welcome on our land."

Decades ago my ancestors helped the fairies settle a dispute that rivaled the Hatfields and McCoys. Those folks were only using shotguns and squirrel rifles. Feuding fairies can do a lot more damage than hot lead. I'd sooner cozy up to a keg of dynamite with a lit Zippo lighter than fool with fully charged fairy dust.

"If you two are done socializing," Press growled, repositioning his tie, "we do have an active case here."

Punk more or less snapped to attention and threw a "yes, sir" in Press's direction, but I knew as well as anyone that the vampire frequently visited the Saturday night fairy barn dances.

Press was turned in Chicago, but he's not from up there. The Jacksons have been in the mountains around Miller's Cove as long as any of us. Press went north to find work during the Depression. He wound up on the police force. Six months after he made detective,

Press walked down the wrong alley and his life took a new, immortal direction.

He rapped politely on the hotel room door and said, "It's Chief Jackson, Mrs. Reynolds."

A woman's voice said, "Come in."

Frank, who had been hovering behind me, asked, "Do you think they'll give Vanessa half the room rate back since it's no longer a double occupancy?"

When I shot him a warning look, the cheapskate fell silent and followed us inside.

Vanessa Reynolds was a dead ringer for Jessica Rabbit. You know, from that movie *Who Framed Roger Rabbit*? He was exactly what the name implies—a rabbit. She was a sultry starlet in an evening dress with a slit right up to what my mama would have called "her business."

Jessica's signature line, "I'm not bad. I'm just drawn that way," was written for botox-plumped lips like the ones Vanessa Reynolds sported. I'd bet good money that red hair came out of a bottle and that her other...assets...were silicone based.

While Press introduced me, I stole a quick look around the room. The Nostalgia Nook toes the period line closely, even installing those vibrating beds with coin boxes attached to the head boards.

Glancing in the open closet door, I saw that the Reynolds came prepared. Proper vintage clothes hung on the attached hangers, but Frank died in his regular modern attire. Interesting.

I came back to myself when I heard the word "assistant" come out of Press's mouth. Twin impulses instantly warred in my system. Pleasure and pique.

Don't get me wrong. I'd be more than happy to assist Press anytime, but why do men always have to go with the "assistant" story to explain a woman's presence in a professional setting?

When I mumbled something about being sorry for Vanessa's loss, the widow dabbed a mascara stained tissue at her now suspiciously dry eyes and flopped into a chair in the seating area by the window.

Press and I took opposite ends of the couch as Vanessa moaned melodramatically, "This just can't be happening to me. How could Frank do this *to me?*"

Her late husband, who had taken up position at the end of one of the beds, let out a protesting squawk. "*Hey!* I'm the one with a hatchet sticking out of my head."

Even if his wife could have heard him, I'm not sure she would have cared. Clearly Vanessa saw Frank's death as a tremendous inconvenience—to her.

As I listened, Press walked her through the timeline of the couple's arrival in Miller's Cove. The duo flew into Nashville two days earlier to catch a performance of the Grand Ole Opry, which Vanessa described acidly as, "Frank's dream. Not my thing."

They then rented a car and drove east for a long weekend in Miller's Cove, which was, according to the widow, her idea. She waxed rhapsodic about the glamour of the 1940s, waving a manicured hand in the direction of several evening dresses in the closet.

The Nostalgia Nook requires guests dress for dinner and the town has three night clubs—one specifically remodeled to look like Rick's in *Casablanca*. She picked the right spot to indulge her fashion fantasy.

The Reynolds arrived in town the day before in time to dine at the lodge, but Frank pleaded fatigue. "He didn't want to change into the right kind of clothes," Vanessa lamented. "If he'd just done what I told him to do, this might not have happened."

From his perch on the bed Frank muttered, "Like I haven't heard that before."

Pointing at the television set with its round screen, Vanessa said, "He took one look at that thing and fell in love. It only shows black and white pictures, can you imagine? We have a 55" high-definition set at home and he wanted to watch ancient movies on a black and white fish bowl."

In defense of the Nostalgia Nook, the TVs they provide are reproductions. The sets default to the on-property vintage streaming service, but if Vanessa had bothered to read the directions, the couple could have watched anything they liked on a *colored fish bowl.*

"We ordered room service so Frank could drool over a bunch of old gangster movies. I fell asleep."

Press, who had been jotting the details of her story in a notebook perched on his knee with a mother-of-pearl fountain pen I would have killed for, said, "What time did he leave the room for ice?"

Vanessa's brow furrowed. "I sort of remember hearing him go out, but I don't know the time. It must have been late. I fell right back to sleep."

"When did you realize he hadn't returned?"

"Early this morning. He wasn't here and neither was the ice bucket. The TV was still on. I would have called his cell phone, but he didn't take it with him." She pointed toward the dresser.

I saw an iPhone next to a set of keys and a cylindrical black object. It wasn't until I looked at the reflection of the items in the mirror mounted at the back of the piece of furniture that I understood what I was seeing—a black jeweler's loupe. I made a mental note to ask Frank about the peculiar item.

As I started to return my gaze to the not-so-grieving widow, something else caught my eye. Five long thin scratches in the veneer of the dresser. The parallel pattern of the marks struck me as familiar, but I didn't know why.

The damage seemed out of keeping with the overall state of the room. Every inch of wood in the place gleamed. Since the scratches hadn't yet fallen prey to a thick coat of furniture polish, they had to be fresh.

The keys could have been the culprit, but the marks weren't jagged or random enough for that to be the case. Normally I wouldn't do something quite as blatant as what I had in mind sitting five feet from a potential murder suspect, but those scratches intrigued me.

Faking a cough, I brought out my equally fake pocketbook phone. Press shot me a warning look, which I chose to ignore. The case actually does have a working pocket on one side, from which I extracted a tissue to cover my mouth.

Ratcheting the cough to a tubercular level, I rasped out, "Press, may I get a glass of water?"

What was the man going to say? *"No. Choke to death?"*

"Use one of the glasses still wrapped in paper," he commanded, "and don't touch anything but the pitcher."

Those would be the glasses sitting right next to the scratches. Perfect.

I crossed the room, pocketbook still in hand, poured myself a tepid glass of water, and in the process took a quick burst of photos of the suspicious marks and the contents of Frank Reynolds's pockets.

When I returned to the sofa I offered a demure apology before reclaiming my seat. From the look in Press's eyes, we would be discussing my charade sooner than later.

We were treated to an account of Vanessa coming upon the body and screaming for help. "The staff brought me right back here," she said. "They were so concerned that I not be traumatized any further."

That might have been true, but I knew they also wanted to gain control of the optics of the killing as quickly as possible. If nothing else, we are good at cover ups in Miller's Cove to keep everything nice and sparkly for the visitors from the outside who pay our bills.

Switching to deeper dive questions, Press said, "What did your husband do for a living, Mrs. Reynolds? Did he have any business acquaintances who might be enemies?"

In the vampire's mind all "business acquaintances" keep men with names like Louie the Hook on retainer for indelicate negotiations.

Vanessa instantly affected unconvincing ignorance. "I really don't know what Frank did. Something to do with imports."

When she said the word Frank flinched, a reaction that sent a thousand possibilities careening through my brain. "Importers" can handle anything from drugs to stolen art. All endeavors worthy of winding up dead.

Press didn't like the answer either. When he wrapped up the interview, I knew he planned to come at Vanessa again after digging deeper into her husband's business affairs.

"We'll let you get some rest, Mrs. Reynolds. I'm sure I don't need to tell you that you shouldn't leave town."

"Of course not, Chief Jackson."

The hussy had the nerve to bat her eyelashes at my vampire when she purred those words. Oh yeah. Vanessa Reynolds was definitely at the top of my suspect list.

As Press and I moved toward the door, I looked at Frank and gave him what I hoped was an imperceptible head jerk intended to telegraph, *"Come on."*

The ghost shook his head.

When I repeated the move, the spook still responded with a silent no and even backed up on the bedspread to put more distance between us.

Since I hadn't yet introduced myself to Vanessa as her dead husband's personal ghost whisperer, I had no choice but to leave Frank in the room.

Once we were outside, Press said, "Okay, spill. What does your client have to say about that conversation?"

"I can't tell you."

Giving me his best insta-scowl, Press said, "Can't or won't?"

"Can't. Frank refused to come with us when we left the room."

Reaching up to loosen his tie again, Press said, "Something's not right about that guy."

Like I hadn't figured that part out already.

Chapter 5

"WHAT'S WITH YOU AND the tie at half mast?" I asked as we walked away. "Are you going for casual and dangerous?"

Without missing a beat, Press said, "More like itching and healing."

Ouch. Not a topic that would keep me in his good graces. Press didn't give me a chance to respond anyway, which is good, because in my heartfelt chagrin at almost frying the man to a crisp, my usual well of snappy comebacks ran dry.

"What about you?" he demanded. "You were auditioning for the remake of *Camille* in there."

I drew a blank on the reference. He tried again. "Alexandre Dumas novel? 1936 Garbo movie? Pretending to cough blood into your Kleenex?"

That's a vampire for you. Always go for the blood. "There were scratches on the dresser. And a jeweler's loupe. I wanted to get photos."

"You saw all that from across the room?"

"I saw all that reflected in the mirror. You remember reflections, don't you, Press?"

"That no-reflection in the mirror bull is myth and you know it. Let me see those pictures."

If he hadn't been so damned good looking I might have told him to take his myth and shove it. Instead, I stopped and handed him my phone, watching as he pinched the screen to enlarge the images.

Try as he might, Press couldn't hide the interest peeking through the scowl on his face, but he didn't intend to give me so much as an inch.

"It's a hotel room, Mattie. The furniture is going to get scratched up. Reynolds probably did it when he tossed his keys down. The loupe is interesting though. Send me those photos."

Again with the command voice. Would he have choked on a "please?" The bill had come due on his attitude.

"Share and share alike, Press. I'll send you my photos if you give me a look at the pictures Jerry took along with the autopsy report."

By this time we'd started moving again. "Brace yourself," the vampire growled. "Cause of death was an ax to the head."

I didn't even cut my eyes in his direction. Press didn't answer for at least a dozen steps. Then he blew out an exasperated blast of air and said, "Fine. Come down to the station tomorrow morning at 9 and you can see what we have. Any chance you won't be late?"

"Very funny," I said as we rounded the corner in time to see Santos and a technician lift Frank's body onto a gurney. Rigor had set in, so they placed the body on its side. I could hear people in the crowd making jokes about how ridiculous "the dummy" looked.

The tourists thought the corpse was a mannequin, which was good, but I have to admit that the longer I knew the deceased, "dummy" wasn't a bad descriptive.

Santos spotted Press. "My guys are going to sack up the ice and take the machine downtown. I don't want to miss any evidence that might be inside."

"Good idea," Press said. "I'm on my way to interview the manager."

Since he didn't include me in that statement, I figured I'd pushed my luck enough with the vampire for one day. Press didn't expect what happened next. It might have been my imagination, but I thought I saw a glimmer of disappointment cross his face. If it reached his eyes, I couldn't tell because his shades were firmly back in place against the offending sunlight.

"Thank you for letting me tag along, Press. I better get back to the shop before Uncle Grim has a fit. See you tomorrow."

With that, I headed across the parking lot toward my car. The weight of Press's suspicious gaze followed me every step of the way.

Once behind the wheel with the engine and the AC running, I glanced at my phone. Lunch time. Punching a number into the device, I waited until a woman's voice said, "Bygone Beauty, Raylene speaking."

"Hey, it's me. Feel like meeting me for lunch at the Deja Vu?"

My best friend's rich, raspy voice came across the line with enthusiasm. "Hey, sugar. You bet. I'm dying to get out of this place. What time?"

"Now if you can get away."

"I'm the boss. Of course I can get away."

"Okay, I'm out at the Nostalgia Nook so you'll get their first. Grab our usual table."

A beat of silence came over the line. "Grapevine says there was an incident out at the Lodge last night."

"More like early this morning. The ghost showed up in the alley behind the shop asking for help when I pulled in. I'll tell you everything over the daily special."

If you're going to get to know me, then you have to know Raylene. She befriended me in the first grade lunch line by marching up and declaring, "Sugar, we have to do something about your fashion sense."

I was six. I didn't even know what fashion sense was, but I knew instantly that the scrawny, too-tall girl with black braids would always have my back.

Raylene needed no guidance in choosing her anachronistic persona. She went straight for that place where Eve Arden, Rosalind Russell, and Thelma Ritter meet Lucille Ball.

If your light on your Hollywood references think brash, big-hearted, lovable broads with husky contralto voices, which, in a pinch, they wielded like straight razors.

A fellow witch and ardent admirer of legendary costume designer Edith Head, Raylene runs the Bygone Beauty Salon one block down from the clock shop. She specializes in glamor and fashion magic, raking in a healthy profit from the female tourists.

Those women slump in the front door of Raylene's place sporting various shades of frump and confusion. They walk out coiffed, confident and captivating—at least for the duration of their stay in Miller's Cove.

Raylene and I have a permanent lease on the corner table at the Deja Vu Diner. The booths that bank the front wall match the red leather, chrome-trimmed barstools and each one comes outfitted with a personal jukebox.

By the time I slid onto the bench seat across from Raylene, our speaker was playing Benny Goodman. My friend had pulled her hair back that day leaving a fringe of bangs in front.

She wore a smart suit in forest green belted at the waist. A bejeweled leopard pin crawled down the left lapel, one front paw extended. Raylene adores big blingy brooches.

"I ordered you the BLT lunch special before Rosie ran out of good lettuce," she said by way of greeting. "Did some guy really get cut up in pieces and stuffed in the ice machine at the Nostalgia Nook?"

Rolling my eyes, I said, "No pieces. One blow to the head, but the killing did happen at the ice machine."

Rosie the one-woman waitress dynamo showed up with a glass of iced tea for me and two BLT plates balanced precariously on her forearm.

As she slid our food onto the table she said, "Mel made chocolate pies this morning. I put two slices back for you gals so save some room." Then, leaning down, she whispered, "I hexed the calories out so don't worry about your diets."

There are perks to being a Deja Vu regular.

While we ate, I filled Raylene in on the morning's event. For the most part she chewed and listened, but when I got to the part about

Press standing under the awning waiting for me she said, "He's speaking to you?"

Spearing a French fry with my fork, I said, "More or less, and he only reminded me about the burns once."

"That's progress."

"True, and he let me go with him to interview the widow." I finished my story with an explanation about how Frank refused to leave the hotel room and then used the most explosive phrase in my repertoire. "I have an idea."

Instantly suspicious, Raylene said, "Those words do not inspire confidence."

"No, really, this will be fine," I assured her. "How about we get gussied up and go back out to the Lodge for dinner tonight? I want to get a good look at everyone who's staying there and maybe ask the manager a few questions without Press around to get in the way."

Raylene dabbed at her mouth, careful not to get lipstick on the white linen napkin. "Well, I never turn down a good gussy up, but what makes you think the killer is still in town?"

Anyone else would have scoffed when I said I had a gut feeling, but Raylene has intimate experience with my gastrointestinal hunches. She'll be the first to tell you we've always gotten into much worse trouble ignoring my gut than going along with it.

We agreed over chocolate pie that I would come to the Bygone Beauty between 5 and 5:30. That alone should tell you that Raylene is a good friend. She doesn't hold me to exact times she knows I can't keep.

"I'll call and make the reservation," she said, downing the last of a cup of black coffee Rosie had delivered along with our dessert. "Be thinking about what kind of outfit you want me to conjure up."

Considering the statement, I said, "I think this job calls for a Bette Davis vibe, but I'll let you know."

Even though we were in walking distance of the salon I gave Raylene a ride back to her place. I don't like to leave the Dodge parked on Main Street. I protect my baby with heavy anti-dent magic, after a reckless visitor bumped her front left fender last winter. Once dinged, twice shy.

Uncle Grim hadn't expected me back for the day, but he didn't turn down my help when I walked in the back door. He repairs antique clocks and watches from all over the United States and far prefers to be at his work bench than dealing with customers.

Retail wise, I had a good afternoon, moving a rare World War II Bulova pilot's watch and a 14k white gold Longines. When I locked the front door at 5:10 and flipped the "Closed" sign over, Grim barely glanced up.

"Raylene and I are going out to the Nostalgia Nook for dinner," I said. "Don't be worried if I'm late."

Staring into the workings of the same pocket watch he'd been rebuilding that morning, Grim said, "Don't get chopped up in pieces and stuffed in the ice machine."

"Oh for Hecate's sake," I said. "There were no pieces."

"Not what I hear," my uncle murmured. "Enjoy your dinner."

He lapsed back into a near-comatose state of concentration. I let myself out and moved the Dodge down to Raylene's back door, using our secret knock to signal my arrival at the beauty shop.

Within seconds, Raylene ushered me inside with, "So, are we doing *Dark Victory* or are you in more of a *Now, Voyager* frame of mind?"

Good movies—1939 and 1942 respectively. Both Oscar nominations for Bette, but I had something else in mind. "*Old Acquaintance*," I replied. "The dress at the end."

Raylene's face lit up. "The chiffon number with the sequin waist and trimmed surplice neckline. Orry-Kelly, not Edith, but still a nice call."

Moving me in front of a leaning floor mirror, Raylene directed me to stand still. I did as I was told. She formed an open-topped square with her thumbs and forefingers. Tiny charges of electricity arced across the frame. I resisted the urge to wiggle as she passed the design hex over my body. Couture magic tickles.

I didn't hear the incantation so much as feel the spell erase my trousers and blouse, replacing them with a lovely drape of champagne chiffon accented with gold sequins. The color made my blue eyes sparkle.

"Twirl for me," Raylene instructed.

She watched me with a critical eye, then snapped her fingers. My hair slid out of the roll at the nape of my neck, assumed a new side part, and fell perfectly over my shoulder in a cloud of thick curls.

Looking down, I saw a gold clutch purse in my hand. When I opened the latch, my phone lay nestled inside along with a compact, and a tube of lipstick in a perfect, complementary shade.

While I touched up my make-up, Raylene stared into the floor mirror, snapping her fingers like castanets. Evening dresses flashed on and off her lean frame like strobe lights until she settled on a classic black gown with a full skirt and a scalloped neck.

A diamond brooch relieved the severity of the monochrome outfit. She finished the look with immaculate Marcel waves in her hair before asking, "What do you think?"

"Perfection."

"That's my specialty," she said with saucy elan. "Now, let's go catch a killer."

"We're going to catch filet mignon," I replied as we exited the salon. "We don't catch the killer until I catch the widow's checkbook."

Frank might not be talking to me, but I was willing to bet Vanessa would have a great deal to say when she found out that her inconveniently dead husband had not left the building.

Chapter 6

FOR ALL ITS RUSTIC charm, the Nostalgia Nook transforms at night. When we pulled under the covered front entrance, a liveried attendant rushed to the passenger side to open Raylene's door while the head valet offered me his hand.

Stepping out of the car, I took the paper ticket he offered. "Hey, Jimmy. When did you get promoted?"

"Last month," he said, turning his head to stifle a sneeze. "No more running all over the parking garage finding people's cars for me. Give me another six months and I'll be the concierge. That means working inside all the time."

Beside me, Raylene said, "We're pulling for you, Jimbo. When your Mama comes in for her permanent this week I'll brag on how well you're doing out here."

Blushing to the roots of his sandy hair, Jimmy thanked her and held the door so we could enter the lobby.

"You know his people don't approve of him working here," Raylene whispered as we crossed a jigsaw of Persian rugs on our way to the main restaurant. "They've put so much pressure on the poor boy."

Glancing at the clock over the lobby fireplace, I saw the big hand sliding past 6:30, the appointed time of our reservation. "We can talk about whatever Jimmy's people have against the Nostalgia Nook when we're seated. For once, *you're* going to make us late."

Raylene kept right on talking like she hadn't heard a word. "You know druids. Everything has to be all oak trees and long white beards."

Resigning myself to her snail's pace, I said, "Be nice. The Owens are good people, just kind of outdoorsy. It isn't easy being the only Druid family in the county. What did they expect Jimmy to do with his life?"

"Get a job with the forest service and work in the national park."

She meant the Cherokee National Forest, which straddles the line between Tennessee and North Carolina. The forest encompasses 655,598 acres. Buckshot Leonard and the other members of the local werewolf pack love to spend full-moon weekends in the more isolated regions where they can howl to their heart's content without worrying about getting shot.

"Jimmy couldn't take a job like that," I said. "He has the worst allergies I've ever seen."

As if to confirm the assertion, a mighty sneeze sounded from the direction of the front door.

"His Mama isn't happy about that either," Raylene confided. "Every time she comes in to get her hair done she complains about him relying on allergy shots instead of meditating his way through the pollen."

I didn't have a chance to offer an opinion on anti-allergy meditation. As we approached the door to the restaurant, the Lodge's maître d' greeted me by name. "Mattie, you look simply ravishing tonight. No doubt one of your creations, Raylene?"

"My take on an Orry-Kelly design," she answered. "How are you, Remi?"

Remi D'Aboville smiled, his perfect teeth gleaming in an immaculate, snowy Van Dyke beard. "I am in the hills, therefore I am a happy man. You are early, but your table is ready."

"Man" being a relative term since Remi is a Barbgazi, a mountain creature that sits somewhere on the evolutionary chart between dwarf and gnome.

Tall for his race, Remi cuts a dapper figure at 5'5". Apart from an obsession with snow and his abnormally large feet, currently encased in gleaming Italian leather, nothing gives away Remi's true identity.

Cutting my eyes toward my companion, I said, "I thought our reservations were at 6:30."

"No," Remi assured me. "Raylene specifically asked for 7 o'clock. Is there a problem?"

"Not at all," I assured him, giving Raylene a pointed look. I guess I couldn't blame anyone for lying to my chronically late self about scheduled appointments.

Remi personally showed us to our table and placed menus in our hands. Champagne cocktails arrived seconds later. "Compliments of the house," Remi said. "May I take the liberty of ordering filet mignon to your individual tastes?"

"You know us too well," Raylene said, surrendering her menu unopened. "We'll leave dinner up to you."

The Barbgazi beamed and went off to undoubtedly order more food than we could eat. I picked up my glass and sipped the expensive champagne, allowing my eyes to roam over the room.

Over the rim of her cocktail, Raylene said, "Vampire at 2 o'clock. Don't look."

Of course, I looked—in the wrong direction.

I never know when someone does the clock face navigation thing if they mean from their perspective or mine. When I finally did get my bearings, the satin lapels of a double-breasted dinner jacket filled my entire field of vision.

Directing my gaze up the expanse of starched white shirt and along a trail of jet studs, I found my way to a perfect bow tie under a chiseled chin belonging to Preston Jackson.

Aware that we were in public, Press reached for my hand, which he kissed, and said, "Imagine meeting you here, Mattie," before repeating the same gallant gesture with Raylene.

"Preston Jackson you look like a movie star," she gushed. "Join us."

The cool touch of the vampire's lips against my skin stopped my mental gears dead, but some functioning part of my brain kicked in and told my mouth to say, "Please do."

Taking an empty chair from a nearby table, Press sat and motioned to a waiter. "May I get a Sidecar and another round for the ladies, please."

As the man scurried away, Press leaned back and crossed his legs. "So, Mattie, you're going to snoop no matter what I say, aren't you?"

With the sun safely below the horizon, Press's mood had improved. Feeling reasonably confident he was teasing me, I felt safe engaging in some verbal sparring.

"Snoop is a harsh word. Raylene and I felt like a girl's night out."

Press arched an eyebrow. "Of course you did. At the lodge where your client was murdered. Is he here, by the way?"

I'd been on the lookout for Frank since Raylene and I entered the building, but to be thorough, I scanned the room. "Nope. I haven't seen him since we talked to Vanessa."

Pretending to flick a bit of lint off the knee of his trousers, Press said, "As it happens, the lady in question has a reservation tonight...for two."

That sent my eyebrows up. "She's having dinner in public with someone the night after her husband was axed at the ice machine?"

Raylene made a judgmental tsking noise. "Well, that sure didn't take her long."

"Exactly," Press agreed, "and it shouldn't take us long to find out the identity of her dinner partner. According to Remi, they should be here any minute. I was hoping to get Frank's reaction to their grand entrance."

Normally I would keep my client's personal information confidential, but since Frank wasn't playing by the rules, I decided to bend them a bit myself. "This morning on our way out here Frank told me he didn't expect Vanessa to take long lining up husband number six.

I wonder if that was his way of telling me he suspected someone was already waiting in the wings?"

In a moment of great service and lousy timing the waiter arrived just then with the fresh drinks, managing to completely block our view of the door. When he finally got out of the way, I spotted Remi leading Vanessa Reynolds and a man to a table near the dance floor.

The guy's back was to me, but when they sat, I recognized Frank. Was the woman possibly in so much denial she made a dinner reservation that included her dead husband?

Using my cocktail glass as a prop to obscure the motion, I lifted my index finger in the direction of the new arrivals. "Scratch that. I can tell you where my client is after all. He just sat down with Vanessa. Third table from the bandstand on the right."

Press and Raylene both looked in the direction I indicated, easily spotting Vanessa who was wearing a bright scarlet evening dress complete with long, black satin gloves and a diamond bracelet.

The woman's flaming hair fell over her bare shoulders and when she leaned forward, nothing was left to the imagination of anyone watching—which included every living man in the place and the dead one sitting beside me.

"Huh," Press said. "At least I can see the guy now, which will make having a conversation with him a heck of a lot easier."

Before I could respond, Raylene said, "Hold your horses, you two. Since when can ghosts flip through menus and drink water?"

She wasn't wrong. Not only did the dead man take a long drink of water, he was conversing with Remi over the wine list.

Putting his drink on the table, Press said, "We need to get a closer look at those two. May I have this dance, Mattie?"

The logical part of my gray matter thought, "*Good plan to get us across the room,*" while the rest shouted, "*He wants to dance with me!*" Thankfully I didn't turn the table over getting to my feet.

Stepping into the circle of Press's arms I placed my hand in his as the band struck up a nice foxtrot, "Any Old Time." They were using the Artie Shaw arrangement with bright, brassy trumpet accents and a killer clarinet solo.

Billie Holiday had done the original vocals. I knew the opening lines by heart. *"Any old time you want me, I am yours, for just the asking, darling. Any old time you need me, I'll be there."*

Crimson heat crept over my cheeks as I thought about the lyrics.

"Is it too hot in here for you?" Press asked. "You're turning red."

"Champagne makes me flush," I lied, following his strong lead around the floor. "You're good at this."

To my surprise he chuckled. "When I was on the force in Chicago, I moonlighted at an Arthur Murray Dance Studio. They always needed someone to dance with the single women."

"Dance with them or chase them?" I teased.

The chuckle turned into a laugh, a deep baritone rumble I felt in my chest. "Arthur Murray was a hunting ground for old maids. I did more dodging than chasing. Get ready. We're on approach to make contact."

I wasn't ready at all if talking to Vanessa and Frank meant I had to turn loose of my partner, but then Press was saying, "Good evening, Mrs. Reynolds. How are you?"

With my left arm lightly encircling Press's waist, I turned to join the conversation when a flash of purple caught my attention near the curtains. The floor-to-ceiling drapes covering the windows that overlooked the mountains were drawn, but for an instant, I thought I saw something duck under the fabric.

When I looked closer, however, the material seemed perfectly still. Assuming my eyes were playing tricks on me, I trained my attention on Vanessa who was saying, "Good evening Chief Jackson. I just could *not* stay in that hotel room all alone and be sad with pretty new clothes hanging in the closet. Frank wouldn't have wanted that and Floyd agreed."

Her dinner companion stood and held out his hand to Press. "Floyd Reynolds. Vanessa told me how kind you've been. Thank you."

Remembering his manners, Press said, "Allow me to introduce my assistant, Mattie Tucker."

Floyd offered me his hand, which I accepted, saying, "Forgive me for staring. I didn't realize Mr. Reynolds had a twin."

Even though I knew the man's facial features from my conversations with Frank, when Floyd Reynolds smiled he exuded a confidence and charm his brother lacked.

"Don't worry about it. Happens all the time. Vanessa called me about Frank. I got here as fast as I could to support my sister-in-law."

Uh huh. Why did I think his definition of "support" differed from mine?

Smooth as silk, Press said, "I know having you here will be a great comfort to Mrs. Reynolds. Perhaps we could talk tomorrow. I'd like to get your insights on your brother's unfortunate demise."

"Absolutely. Any time. I have the room right next door to Vanessa's."

As Press and I resumed our dance, I said against his ear, "That's convenient, don't you think?"

"*Too* convenient," he agreed. "Now we *really* need to have a conversation with your client."

He spun me around as he spoke, affording me a perfect view of the newly materialized Frank Reynolds. He was standing—or rather floating—back at the table waving his arms frantically to get my attention.

"That can be arranged," I told Press. "Guess who's coming to dinner?"

Chapter 7

WE FINISHED OUR DANCE and returned to the table. Frank started talking to me as soon as I came within earshot.

"This is too much," the ghost declared, his voice taking on a strident note as his form flickered in and out like a television with a bad tube. "First somebody kills me and now my brother is wearing my clothes and eating dinner with my wife."

Of the three things he mentioned, I couldn't tell which bothered Frank the most. Press held my chair. As I sat, I told Raylene, "Heads up. We have company."

Our dinner had arrived while we were on the dance floor, but Raylene waited to start. Now, picking up her knife and fork, she said, "Ectoplasmic, I assume?"

The ectoplasm I could have handled, but Frank was rapidly working himself into a regular conniption fit. Surveying the seating arrangement, he said, "Oh, I get it. Dead guy has to stand, huh? Do you know what I've found out over the last few hours? The living are rude. *Rude*, I tell you."

Slicing into my filet mignon, I said, "Frank, the first rule of thumb when communicating with a ghost is don't draw the attention of witnesses. Besides, you're talking so loud we couldn't ignore you even if we wanted to."

"Actually we can," Raylene corrected me. "I don't see or hear a thing."

I looked at Press. The vampire shook his head. "Me either. You have Mr. Reynolds all to yourself."

Lucky me.

"So I don't get to sit down," Frank whined. "No one but you is listening to me. At least I'm not the only one getting a taste of your uncouth behavior. You're eating in front of that cop like he isn't even there. This must be hell."

If the ghost kept this up, I'd give him a much clearer view of what an eternity in perdition's flame might look like.

Willing myself not to lose my temper, I relayed the spirit's comments to Press. The vampire sipped at his cocktail and delivered a more effective lecture than anything I might have said.

"Mr. Reynolds, it's also rude to harangue people at the dinner table. I'm a vampire. I take my protein in liquid form. Now how about you settle down and answer some questions before I'm forced to get an exorcist in here and consign you to a much more unpleasant afterlife."

Frank blanched a new shade of pale. "He's a vampire?"

Chasing an errant Brussel sprout around my plate, I said, "He is."

"Could he really have someone send me to someplace awful?"

"I don't know, would you like to risk finding out?"

That did it. Instant contrition. "I'll be glad to answer the nice policeman's questions."

"You're now a nice policeman," I told Press. "Fire away with the questions."

The vampire shifted in his chair. "Sorry about this, Raylene."

"No need to apologize," she said, buttering a fresh roll. "This is better than charades. Besides, I want to hear how Vanessa hooked up with a dead ringer for her husband." Then, thinking about her phrasing, she added, "No offense on the dead part, Frank."

"None taken," the ghost said, his eyes on his wife and brother across the room. "That rat's my identical twin."

Raylene let out a low whistle at that news. "That is some majorly dirty pool."

Press, armed with a fresh Sidecar, funneled questions through me. Frank turned out to be a veritable fount of information.

Floyd Reynolds had arrived at the Nostalgia Nook that morning moments after Press and I left Vanessa. He parked his rental car in the garage, checked in, and requested the room next door to his sister-in-law as a "bereavement" courtesy.

The manager, anxious to keep the murder quiet, agreed and had Floyd's bags taken up while Floyd himself joined Vanessa. The pair spent the afternoon talking before deciding to dress and come down to dinner.

"Did they say anything incriminating?" Press asked.

"No," the ghost said. "They used code words and gestures."

When I reported that information Raylene asked, "Why would they do that? Weren't they alone in the room?"

"Vanessa was obsessed with the dresser," Frank said. "When Floyd arrived she put a finger to her lips to signal him to be quiet, then led him over there and pointed before she put both hands behind her ears like she was trying to hear something."

"She thinks we bugged the room," I said. "She was telling Floyd not to say anything important because someone might be listening."

Frank confirmed my suspicion. "When they were walking down to dinner Vanessa told my brother she knew you had to have been up to something when you went over to get a drink of water. She said she never heard such a phony cough in her whole life."

Press started to laugh, but a look from me stopped him. Instead he said, "Why would your wife be nervous about listening devices?"

"Gee, I don't know," Frank shot back with dripping sarcasm. "Maybe she's not anxious for anyone to find out that she's fooling around with my brother."

The vampire's next question was the one we were all thinking. "Are your wife and brother capable of planning and executing a murder?"

"No," Frank said. "Floyd's number one reason for living is to torture me. Killing me would ruin his fun. Vanessa can't stand the sight of blood and…"

His voice trailed off. I recognized the confused reaction. "Are you remembering something, Frank?"

"When I got to the ice machine I saw a weird shadow," he said, the words coming out with a jerky, uncertain cadence. "The shadow went away really fast, so I didn't think much about it, but right before everything went black, the back of my neck started to itch."

Raylene frowned. "Does he mean he felt like he was being watched?"

"No," Frank answered. "My neck itched like something was crawling on me."

"I'll have Santos check the back of the corpse's neck," Press said, taking a notebook out of the breast pocket of his jacket.

"*Hey!*" Frank protested. "That's my body you're talking about. Show some respect."

Given the previous threat of exorcism, I decided not to pass that comment along to Press.

Through the rest of dinner Frank kept his eyes glued to Vanessa and Floyd. The couple didn't do anything but eat and listen to the music. They got up to leave as soon as they'd had coffee.

On their way past us, Floyd's appearance caused a mild stir. A man at a nearby table said, "Great performance this morning, buddy. You deserve an Oscar."

The tourists still believed what they'd witnessed had been a show for their benefit with actors. Floyd didn't have a clue what the people were talking about, but he acknowledged their compliments with polite thanks.

When we stood to leave, Frank said, "What am I supposed to do? Can I come home with you?"

"No you can't," I said firmly. "I do not allow clients in my home and the property is warded. You couldn't get in anyway."

Press, understanding the exchange without hearing it, said, "Tell him to keep an eye on his wife and brother for us."

I looked at Frank who said, "I'm dead, not deaf. I heard him. You better give me a discount for doing your job for you." With that, he blinked out of sight.

Press walked us to our car. On the way, I described Frank's parting shot to me.

"Oh, he's a real winner, that one, " Raylene said. "Are you sure this case is worth it? I'm not seeing a paycheck in this for you, Mattie."

"Give me time," I assured her. "Frank may be a jerk, but that's all the more reason to help him move along. The last thing I want is for him to become a permanent resident in Miller's Cove. Besides, now I'm intrigued about what Vanessa and Floyd are really doing out here."

"That makes two of us," Press said, holding the car door for me. "I'm going to the piano bar for a night cap and see if I can pick up any scuttlebutt from the staff. The tourists might be clueless, but I'm sure there's plenty of in house gossip circulating. See you in the station in the morning, Mattie. Good night, Raylene."

She wished him a good night, I gave Jimmy a generous tip, and pointed the nose of the Dodge toward town. The wheels weren't even off the property before Raylene said, "I can't believe you didn't wrangle an invite to go to the piano bar with him."

"I'm trying to get on his good side," I said. "Not just because of the case but because, well, you know."

"Yeah, I know. I was watching that dance you two shared. You were so flustered you turned beet red."

"God," I groaned, "was it that obvious?"

"No more obvious than you being head over heel for Mr. Tall, Pale, and Broody."

Anxious to change the subject, I said, "What did you think about Vanessa Reynolds?"

"She's guilty."

"What makes you say that?"

"The wife is always guilty. Besides, if you were married to Frank, wouldn't you kill him?"

We both laughed. "I'd like to think I might *want* to kill him but wouldn't go through with it."

"If I know my dames," Raylene said, "and I think I do, Vanessa is definitely hiding something and Floyd sure as heck isn't here to be a supportive brother-in-law."

We drove a mile or two in silence and then I said, "Did you notice anything strange in the dining room?"

Raylene thought for a minute. "Yeah, come to think of it, I did. They've changed the lighting or something in there. I kept seeing moving shadows out of the corner of my eye."

"What color were they?"

She frowned, "Shadow colored?"

"That's a lot of help. I could have sworn I saw something purple duck under the curtains over the back windows."

"There was a woman in the room wearing a purple cocktail dress," Raylene said. "Really bad cut for her figure and cheap material. You probably caught a glimpse of her."

Unlike Raylene, who is a walking fashion monitor, I hadn't paid a bit of attention to what anyone else in the restaurant was wearing other than Vanessa.

Still, the answer seemed plausible enough so I accepted it, but not without hearing that wise little voice in the back of my head declare, *"Yeah, that's not what you saw."*

I filed that doubt away for later examination. After I dropped Raylene off at her house, I drove home to the elegant old Craftsman bungalow I inherited from my parents.

Uncle Grim lives in an apartment over the detached garage. His lights were off, so I left the Dodge in the driveway rather than awaken my uncle pulling up the garage door.

Passing through the wards that protect the privacy of my home, I used an incantation to open the magical lock on the front door. Leaving my bag on the hall table, I went upstairs to change.

I found the slacks and blouse I'd worn that day neatly laid out on the chaise in my bedroom, cleaned and newly pressed. That's my girl Raylene. She never misses a beat.

Changing into silk pajamas and slippers, I went back downstairs to make tea before heading to the den. The night was still young. I had some detecting to do.

Chapter 8

———◈———

ARMED WITH A STEAMING cup of Earl Grey, I went into the room that had been my father's study. I spend more time there than in any other spot in the house. During the summer months, a set of fake electric logs light the fireplace—technically a breach of period etiquette, but a girl has to do what ambiance demands.

I put the cup down beside the easy chair that had been in the family for generations and switched on one of my most prized possessions after the Dodge: a 1932 General Electric J-100 cathedral radio. She pre-dates FM by four years, but the Miller's Cove radio station simulcasts on AM and FM.

You may be wondering if the people of my town function completely without an awareness of modern conveniences and technology. Clearly since I rely on an iPhone like most of the rest of the world, the short answer is no. But our relationship with modernity here in Miller's Cove involves more nuanced shades of complexity.

Since the community's transformation as the South's premier nostalgia destination, we've all become less wedded to the 21st century even in the privacy of our homes where no one's watching. For some locals who were born in the 18th century, the step back didn't prove difficult at all.

Sticking with the wisdom that a lady does not reveal her age, I'll only tell you that I'm a 20th century model, but one with a pre-existing appreciation for old-fashioned things. Slowly, however, the life I lived in public to keep pace with the town's new theme became less an act and more my primary existence.

The gradual trend solidified into a conscious decision the night Raylene and I went to the "premier" of the film *Jezebel* at the Majestic Memory Palace, our local movie theatre.

The movie was really released in 1938. Bette Davis won her second and last Oscar for her portrayal of spoiled, strong-willed belle Julie Marsden—a consolation prize since Vivian Leigh snagged the plumb women's role of the decade, Scarlett O'Hara.

There I sat with my huge tub of popcorn, Raylene at my side, taking in the newsreels before the feature began. My heart started to thud in my chest over the reports of the rising tide of fascism in Europe—until I remembered the war had come and gone decades before with a definitive win for our side.

At first I found the experience disconcerting, but then I realized the true effect of turning the collective Miller's Cove clock backward. We'd embraced life in a slower time when people were more connected and the line between good and bad could be drawn with greater clarity.

After the *Jezebel* premier I went home and retired my single-cup coffee maker and plastic pods for a percolator that goes on the stove and never looked back. When a gal like me changes her means of brewing caffeinated goodness, you can bet she's embraced a new life direction.

That night however, on the evening after Frank Reynolds's murder, I used a combination of magic and modernity to get to work solving the case. With soft classical music filling the study, I sank into the well-indented chair cushion and took a breath to focus my power.

Then, with a wave of my hand, I lifted the photos I'd taken at the Nostalgia Nook into thin air where they floated between me and the hearth. Sipping my tea, I sorted the images, and spun red gossamer threads to connect points on which I wanted to focus.

Witches don't use white boards.

Duplicating a shot of Frank's body protruding from the ice machine, I zoomed in on the sole of his left shoe. With my index finger,

I sent a glowing red line to encircle a purplish spot on the leather, writing in the air beside the picture, "Ask Press to let me look at the vic's shoes."

When I got to the snapshots of the top of the dresser in Vanessa's room, I stared at those scratches in the wood for almost half an hour. Magnification told me the implement that made the marks was razor sharp and needle thin, but no matter how I rotated the image, I couldn't make out why the pattern seemed so familiar.

I jumped when the announcer's dulcet tones floated out of the radio. "That concludes our musical program for this evening. This is radio MLRS signing off the air."

Tapping the phone's screen with my index finger, I watched the time click over to the first minute of a new day. My cue to turn in and get some sleep. Reaching out with my magic, I folded the diagram in mid-air and drew it back into the phone.

In case you haven't noticed, I don't shop at the same app store you use.

Switching off the lights, I climbed the stairs in semi-darkness and crawled into bed. I think I must have been asleep the instant my head hit the pillow because I spent the remainder of the night dancing with Press in my dreams, but in this version he wore a purple suit with a hatchet lapel pin and the dance floor was an ice rink.

I awakened to a gorgeous day. Sunlight streamed through my bedroom windows and outside the birds offered up a full-throated good morning chorus.

Downstairs in the kitchen, I watched the percolator until coffee bubbled into the glass knob on top. Pouring the heavenly smelling java into a mug, I added cream and sugar. Standing at the sink sipping myself toward consciousness, I waved at Uncle Grim when he glanced my way as he backed the Model A out of the garage and chugged off to work.

After a breakfast of poached eggs and toast, I went upstairs to change. Since it was a Saturday, and I didn't know what I'd be doing that day, I chose a pair of denim trousers with four big buttons on the side, a gold and black checked blouse with three-quarter length sleeves, and sensible Oxfords.

Staring at myself in the mirror, I turned my collar up at a jaunty angle before adding a loosely knotted gold kerchief at my throat. As a final touch, I pulled my hair back and tied it in place with a black ribbon.

The drive to the police station took less than ten minutes. The Dodge's bright blue paint looked out of place sitting with the black and white police cruisers parked out front. Each one sported a single red bubble light on the roof.

Tripping up the steps, I entered the lobby. The desk sergeant, Sam Petrie, called out, "Morning, Mattie. Chief Jackson said for you to come on back."

"Thanks, Sam," I said, starting to push through the double doors only to jump out of the way when the burly figure of Buckshot Leonard burst through the opening.

Before I could say a word, the mayor poked an index finger in my face and said, "*You!* I have a few things to say to you, too."

Caught completely off guard, I stammered, "Good morning, Buckshot."

"Don't you try that good morning stuff with me," he snapped. "I'm going to tell you the same thing I told your boyfriend, murder is not good for this town."

My boyfriend? Did the rest of the town know something I didn't?

Without pausing for breath, Buckshot said, "The both of you need to stop trying to make a big deal out of what happened at the Nostalgia Nook last night. The Lodge is a vital part of the local economy and I will not have the two of you casting suspicions in the minds of the tourists. For all you know Frank Reynolds's death could have been an accident."

Conscious that Sam and every other uniformed officer in the lobby was looking at us, I said, "Really, Buckshot? How exactly did the man fall backward on a hatchet?"

"How do you know that's not exactly what happened?" the mayor demanded. "Were you there? No, I didn't think so. I'm telling you and Press to back off and consider the welfare of this community."

With that, he turned, stalked past me, and stormed out the front door of the station house. My eye fell on the calendar hanging by the entrance to the squad room. One week to the full moon. There's not a female hormone on the planet that can compare to a werewolf gearing up to get furry.

Giving Buckshot the benefit of the doubt, I stepped into the room and came face to face with Jerry Michaels. Since Press was promoted to chief of police, he shouldn't technically be working cases in the field, and Jerry should have been assigned a new partner, but neither had happened.

No one dared suggest to Press that a change might be in order. In my experience, immortals aren't big on change.

Jerry had his coat off and shirtsleeves rolled up. With his fedora pushed high on his head and his service revolver in plain sight in a shoulder holster, he looked like a cop peeled right off the page of a crime novel.

"Hi, Mattie. Did the mayor mow you down on his way out?"

"Not quite," I said, "but he did give me an ear full. Apparently he doesn't think a murder at the Lodge is good for local business."

"Yeah," Jerry said, "we all got that part when he was screaming at Press."

I groaned inwardly. I'd hoped to find the vampire in a good mood even if the sun was up. "How did that go over?"

Jerry laughed. "Buckshot stomped out the front and Press stomped out the back. He said to tell you to come on out there when you got here." As he spoke, he pointed to a door that I knew led to a small, shaded courtyard where Press went to smoke during work hours.

"Thanks, Jerry," I said, starting across the room.

"Oh, and Mattie?"

"Yes?"

"Press said to tell you to think like Vanessa Jackson in the hotel room."

That took a moment to register, but then I got the message. Press wanted me to make sure that no one could overhear our conversation.

Chapter 9

I CLOSED THE DOOR BEHIND me. Press sat in the center of the courtyard on a square concrete bench that enclosed a massive oak tree. The deep shade dropped the temperature to a near chill that made me wish I'd grabbed a light sweater on my way out of the house.

A mostly empty pack of Luckies rested beside the vampire. Like Jerry, Press was in his shirtsleeves, the cuffs rolled up to the elbow. He'd been turned in the prime of his youth. Thick cords of muscle defined his forearms and biceps marked with the faintest hint of the burns I'd accidentally inflicted.

Looking up at the sound of the door, Press put his index finger to his lips, then pointed up and transcribed a circle in the air. I obliged with a privacy cloak and joined him on the bench.

He scooted over to make room for me, tapping ash from his cigarette into the bucket at his feet. "You're late."

That greeting was getting old. "Blame it on His Honor the mayor."

"You saw Buckshot?"

"He almost ran me down in the lobby and then tried to convince me Frank Reynolds tripped and fell backward onto that hatchet."

Press pursed his lips in disapproval. "I've heard the theory."

Taciturn responses weren't moving the conversation forward.

"What's got Buckshot in rabid dog mode? I thought everything was contained at the Lodge. Those people at dinner last night did everything but ask for Floyd's autograph."

The vampire's mouth settled in a grim line. "I believe there's more going on at the Lodge."

This was like pulling fangs. "Such as?"

He removed the last Lucky from the pack, lighting the fresh smoke off the stub of the one in his mouth. We were really going to have to have a conversation about his smoking.

Taking a deep drag, Press said, "I'm about to do something I'll probably regret."

"Okay, I'll bite. What?"

The vampire caught the pun, but didn't react. "Give you complete access to my case. Try not to get me killed, okay?"

For a minute I thought my hearing must be going. Complete access?

Looking back, I realize that in the moment vague disappointment flooded my system mixed with a tinge of fear. Press and I had a well-established dynamic. He growled and told me to mind my business. I refused and drove him nuts.

We sparred verbally and in the process made each other better at our jobs. What would a cooperative version of us look like? And why was I being let into the inner circle now with no effort on my part to knock down the palace gates?

Sure, on a personal level the news thrilled me, but professionally, I wasn't so sure. "Why would you make that offer now?" I said. "I thought I was a pain in your keyster?"

A muscle in Press's cheek twitched. "You are a pain in my keyster and I have the scars to prove it."

Hecate's hat pins! *That* again?

"Press, I didn't know the tanning bed could hurt you. The whole thing was an accident. That psychic made my EMF spike. I can't control that."

The tip of his cigarette flared cherry bright before he exhaled a cloud of blue smoke. "Any more than I can control what happens to me when I'm in direct sunlight too long—even the artificial kind."

"I'm really sorry, Press. I would never do anything to hurt you on purpose."

The vampire leaned forward and rested his forearms on his knees, hands dangling loosely. "I know that, Mattie, which is why I'm doing this. I need a partner I can trust."

My smart mouth went straight to autopilot. "Jerry is your partner."

With a shake of his head Press said, "Dames. Even when I'm giving you something you want, you argue. Jerry is my *official* partner. I'm asking you to be my *unofficial* partner. Are you in or not?"

This time instead of saying the wrong thing my mouth dropped open like a beached trout. Were words like "trust" and "partner" really falling from Preston Jackson's lips?

"I'm in," I stammered. "Definitely in, but I'd still like to know why."

Sitting up, Press shot me a comfortingly familiar annoyed look. "Stop staring at me like a fish out of water and I'll tell you."

On command, my jaws popped shut.

"That's better," Press said. "Buckshot is my boss. He wants me to back off. I have to at least look like I'm following orders until I can put some proof in front of the man and change his mind."

Surely he hadn't said what I thought he said. "*You're* going to back off an investigation?" Maybe that tanning bed fried a few of the vamp's brain cells before I pulled the plug.

With fake patience, Press said, "*Pretend* to back off. I do have a responsibility to this town. We have a good thing going here. Something our ancestors never could have imagined. I don't want to screw that up."

Miller's Cove was settled by transplanted paranormals from all over the South, creatures and species that arrived incognito with the first settlers. Hiding in plain sight is hard work, however. Those pioneers needed a special kind of community to be safe and prosper, which is what brought them to the hollows and coves that surround our town.

Everyone who lives in Miller's cove feels a special connection to the ancestors. All trailblazers are brave, but our forefathers risked everything coming to the New World in the company of humans. They risked exposure and persecution.

I understood what Press was saying, but not how it related to the events at the Nostalgia Nook. "What does the well being of Miller's Cove have to do with Frank Reynolds's death?"

"That," Press said, "is the question I want your help to answer. Reynolds's murder might not draw in unwanted attention from the outside, but what may be going on at the Lodge could."

His words hung in the air between us. Long before the citizens of Miller's Cove agreed to re-invent our community, we already followed an unwritten law. Never let the humans find out the truth about our town.

"You're scaring me," I said. "What happened at the Lodge last night after Raylene and I left?"

Press glanced around. "You're sure no one can hear us?"

"Positive."

"Okay. I had a drink with Remi in the piano bar when the restaurant closed. He suspects someone on the staff is stealing credit card information from the guests and then hexing them to accept the bogus charges."

I swore under my breath, turning the air just blue enough to raise the vampire's eyebrows. Humans will ignore almost anything they can't understand. Accept the most ludicrous, improbable explanations—until someone puts a hand in their pockets.

Sure, we transformed Miller's Cove into a profitable tourist destination to survive in the modern world, but money is the *life blood* of human society. They can and do kill over the stuff. Press would never suggest such a thing was going on until he was reasonably confident in the accuracy of his information.

There was, however, one big problem. The guests at the Nostalgia Nook weren't allowed to use credit cards.

American Express introduced the first charge card in 1958. Letting the plastic to be part of Miller's Cove commerce, at least in an obvious way, pushed the accuracy of the town's timeline.

Most stores, Tucker's Horology included, accept the cards in the name of profit, but at the Lodge every purchase goes on a tab, which is settled at the end of the stay.

When I alluded to the well-known policy, Press said, "Which is exactly what Buckshot came over here this morning to point out—forcefully. The guests themselves enter the card information at the check out and validate the amounts. Staff members don't handle the cards for fear of erasing them."

With good reason. I'm not the only one in town with personal electrical issues. Absent a good coating of barrier magic, I wouldn't dare touch a credit card.

"Then how is the information being stolen?" I asked.

"Remi doesn't know, but he thinks the guests receive an accurate accounting when they leave the Lodge. The bogus charges happen within a week of their departure when the hex kicks in."

"How does he know all that?"

Press explained that a couple of weeks ago a credit card company called about a disputed charge in the restaurant. Remi remembered the party and what they ate. That's why he's good at his job.

When Remi pulled the tab, however, the bill was ten times the correct amount. Before he could confirm the error, however, the card company called back to say the matter had been resolved. The customer had accepted the charges.

The exchange made Remi suspicious so he called the guests to apologize for any inconvenience they might have suffered. In the conversation, he uncovered multiple false memories of the couple's stay at the Lodge.

"After that," Press said, "Remi pulled more records and made more phone calls. Same thing in every case. Sky high bills, which the guests accepted as legit and Remi knew were anything but."

"When was he planning to tell you about all this?"

"The day Frank Reynolds was killed. Remi thinks there might be a connection between the two events and so do I, but we're both just operating on a hunch."

Given how less than forthcoming Frank had been with us in our conversations to date, I understood the suspicion.

"Buckshot wants the murder investigation to go away fast," Press said. "He says if the guests declined to dispute the charges, that's it. Done deal. No problem. I don't buy it. That's where you come in."

"How?"

"You don't face the same constraints I do. Finally, after all these years, your snooping will come in handy."

This time there was no doubt. The corner of the vampire's mouth quirked into a full blown smile—directed squarely at yours truly.

I favored him with a radiant smile in response and tossed out a flirtatious, "I don't snoop."

"Says you," Press tossed back.

Anybody else hearing the words would have heard bemused sarcasm, but Press was playing along with my flirting. That teasing note in his voice clinched what was already a very done deal. I was going to like this new arrangement between us just fine.

"Okay," I said, rubbing my hands together in anticipation. "Where do we start?"

Chapter 10

PRESS FINISHED HIS cigarette. "We go inside, look at the crime scene photos, and then talk to Santos."

Even though the abrupt change in our work relationship pleased me, the lack of resistance from the vampire would require some adjustment on my part.

Recognizing my millisecond of hesitation, Press added, "Or we can argue about what to do next if it would make you more comfortable."

"You," I said, jabbing my index finger at his chest, "are enjoying this entirely too much. Shouldn't we start quietly working the credit card angle, too?"

Then something occurred to me. "Wait a minute. Why did you tell Buckshot about your suspicions before you had proof?"

"I didn't tell him."

"Then who did?"

"No idea. Remi plays his cards close to his vest. Jerry knows, but there's no way he ratted me out to the mayor."

"So Buckshot blew in here out of the blue and started yelling like he knew everything?"

"Yep. He didn't have all the details, but he knew enough to order me to back off."

There could only be one explanation. "Someone at the Lodge is watching Remi. Do you think he could be in danger?"

"I guess that depends on whether or not we find a connection between Frank Reynolds's murder and the fraud. Don't worry about Remi, though. He can take care of himself. I've already asked Jerry to look into the credit card business. He's good with the humans."

Jerry is a siren. Unlike the vengeful creatures in Greek mythology that sang to sailors to make them wreck their vessels against rocky coastlines, Jerry hums and occasionally whistles to ease a situation or to make a witness more talkative.

He's an ethical guy and never abuses his power. Word to the wise, however. Avoid female sirens when they're mad. Shipwrecks will be the least of your worries.

"So you want me to concentrate on Frank's murder?" I asked.

"He did hire you. Working with me doesn't pay."

That depended on a person's definition of "pay."

"I'll be lucky if I get a dime out of Vanessa or Floyd, but that doesn't matter. This credit card scam is a threat to Miller's Cove. That takes priority."

This time Press gave me a smile filled with genuine warmth. "I thought that's how you'd feel. Talk to Remi yourself. Maybe you'll see a potential link between the two crimes that I missed. That's your special skill set, right?"

There's only so many shocks a woman can take in one morning. "Are you all right?" I demanded. "Do you have some fatal vampire disease or something?"

Press rolled his eyes. "Mattie, you can't be a vampire without experiencing a personal fatality. Why?"

"Because we've been running into each other on investigations for years and not once—*not one, single time*—have you ever acknowledged my clue-based powers. What the heck happened to change you?"

I picked up a subtle shift in the energy between us when Press answered me. "I remember what you did after your EMF set off the tanning bed."

His words instantly returned me to the darkened back room of the Reminiscent Riviera. The killer in that case, a shady psychic with an unhealthy interest in her client's financial secrets, tackled me with a wave of telekinetic energy.

Losing my balance, I stumbled into a tanning bed. On contact the machine put out a burst of intense UVA radiation at the exact moment Press and Jerry burst through the door.

People, before you climb into one of those human rotisserie ovens, you might want to remember that the radiation they emit is *three times* as strong as natural sunlight.

Yeah, it's not the light that fries the vamps; it's the radiation. The *cancer-causing* radiation.

Press wears sunscreen, but to my horror under the intense onslaught of the invisible particles pouring out of the machine, his arms and chest burst into flames.

Normally, I can't control my EMF, but that night was different. I reacted without thinking and melted that tanning bed like a s'more. At the same time, I teleported Press and Jerry to Santos's house where the witch doctor saved the vampire's life.

I'd never done anything that magically awesome or desperate. I don't talk about the event because I don't know how I did it, and frankly, that scares me a little.

That was also the first time I tasted my power. Everyday spells are plain vanilla, but that spontaneous burst was an explosion of something more exotic—wild honey, oranges, and smoke.

Which could have been the smoldering tanning bed, but I'm not sure.

Bottom line: rogue powers are rarely a witch's friend until control and discipline enter the equation.

Caught unaware by Press's confession that he remembered more about that night than he'd previously let on, I mumbled, "I thought you were unconscious."

"Nope."

"Then why have you been giving me such a hard time for all these months?"

He grinned. "I'm a complicated kind of undead guy."

For the moment I'd had all the complications I cared to deal with and opted for the mature route out of the uncomfortable conversation—I changed the subject.

"So. About talking to Remi. Punk Jones said the fairies are picking tonight. Remi never misses one of their get-togethers. He may have big feet, but that's one Barbgazi who can cut a rug."

"Perfect," Press said. "The werewolves aren't welcome at the fairy parties after that incident with the garbage cans. Buckshot won't be there to interfere. I might just find my way out to Punk's place, too."

Was it me, or was Press hellbent on *not* discussing business? Fine, two can play. I tossed out a low-level flirtation. "Does that mean I get another dance?"

Press stood, dusted off his hands, and flirted right back. "You know what they say. Anything's possible on fairy land."

Over our heads the branches shifted, throwing dappled light across his pale skin. For an instant I imagined what Press must have looked like in life—tanned, maybe even swarthy. But then the light shifted again and his features resumed their chiseled, alabaster lines.

The vampire caught my lingering gaze. "Something wrong?"

Snapping back to reality, I got to my feet as well. "Sorry. I only took time for one cup of coffee with breakfast. I zoned out there for a minute."

"Well, that won't do. Follow me. Sam throws a rusty horseshoe in the squad room coffee pot before he hits the brew button. That stuff will wake you up. Guaranteed."

He wasn't wrong. My spoon almost stood upright in the potent liquid when I added sugar and stirred. At the first sip I felt energy pulsate through my nervous system. The wave hit my EMF and sent a static bolt arcing over the cup's rim.

"What did you say Sam puts in this stuff?" I asked.

Press shrugged. "I learned a long time ago not to question a kitchen witch. Sure road to heartburn."

I made a mental note to ask Sam for the incantation as I followed Press into the conference room. We trade more than casserole recipes in the paranormal south.

Press and Jerry had turned the conference room into command central for their murder case. Outfitted with a scarred oak table and chairs, the room provided privacy and an enormous cork board covering one wall.

Thumbtacks held an array of black and white photos in place along with other evidentiary documents. A receipt for two tickets to the Grand Ole Opry were pinned up beside a hotel bill from Nashville, a rental car contract, and copies of Frank and Vanessa's drivers licenses.

Press had been checking out the details of the story Vanessa told us during her initial interview.

Taking a closer look at the Opry tickets, I said, "Front row orchestra. Country music really was Frank's thing."

"And clothes and jewelry are Vanessa's. Check out what she spent getting ready to turn back time in Miller's Cove."

He shoved a file folder across the table. I stopped its slide with my hand and flipped back the manila cover. Shuffling through the stack of bills, I let out a two-note whistle.

"I'd like to know what Frank imports to pay for his wife's expensive tastes."

"He's no frugal Freddie in the spending department," Press said, skating another folder across to me.

Studying the contents, I said, "She buys satin and pearls and he picks up glass electrical insulators on eBay?"

"Some of those insulators are $200 a pop. The guy collected all kinds of strange things."

Still reviewing the record of Frank's spending habits, I said, "I think the word you're looking for is 'hoarded.'"

"The Reynolds do make an odd pair. I'd be interested to know how they got together."

"I'll put that on my list of questions for the deceased."

Closing the folder, I returned to the wall of photos. Even though I'd snapped my own images the day before, Jerry had been free to photograph the scene from all angles.

Press pulled out a chair, sat, and leaned back. "Okay. You're good at reading a scene. What do you see?"

Leaning closer, I tapped my finger on a full-on shot of Frank's backside sticking out of the ice machine. "If the vic was scooping ice when the killer struck, shouldn't one of his hands be inside the machine?"

"Very good, but I'll go you one better. There was no ice bucket inside the machine and the scoop was missing."

"So Frank lied."

"Or someone altered the scene."

Staring at the photo, I imagined the sequence of events that might have happened the night of the killing. "It almost looks like Frank grabbed the side of the door to catch himself. I'll ask him about that when I see him. Details like that could job his memory."

"Are you going to the Lodge to track down your client when you leave here?"

"Not directly. I need to check in with Uncle Grim first. Was there anything inside the machine other than ice?"

Press picked up a clipboard and flipped through the pages. "Santos and his boys let the ice melt and strained the liquid through all kinds of filters. Nothing."

"Did they check the soles of the vic's shoes?"

More page flipping. "Well-worn loafers. Nothing remarkable."

"I'm not so sure about that. Look at this stain on the left sole. Does that look purple to you?"

Press couldn't hide his amusement. "Not on a black and white photo it doesn't."

"Oh, sorry."

Taking out my phone, I levitated my working diagram out of the device with a sweeping motion of my fingers and suspended the material on a right angle with the cork board.

That brought Press forward in his chair. "Well, look at you."

I won't lie. His impressed reaction pleased me. "These would be those powers you've been denying I possess."

"My bad," he admitted, "and that's no stock app."

Trying to sound humble and failing, I said, "I've made some improvements in the operating system. It's helpful to keep my notes with me during an investigation. So, here's the shoe sole in color. The angle isn't good, but you can still make out the stain."

Press got up and walked over to take a closer look at the image. "He could have stepped in gum," the vampire suggested.

"I don't think so. Will you have Santos test the stain?"

"Ask him yourself. Let's hit the lab."

Gesturing at the wall of evidence, I said, "Do you mind if I copy all this?"

"Be my guest."

Starting with the cork board, I said, "*Adjunctus.*

One at a time duplicates of the photos peeled off the wall and arranged themselves in sequence with their nearest associates on my diagram.

Moving next to the file folders and clipboard, I switched to a different kind of magic, tapping a rhythm on each item with my forefinger.

When the first folder cloned itself and headed for the phone, Press asked, "What are you doing? Morse code spells?"

"Something like that. Just a trick I came up with so I can work magic in front of humans without attracting attention. There's another sequence to hide the duplication and transit process, but I used an abbreviated version since it's just us in the room."

If Press had any lingering doubts about my methods for processing evidence, I appeared to have erased them. "Since we're working together now," he said, "you're going to need to give me a list of your tools of the trade."

"Maybe I will and maybe I won't," I replied with a wink. "A lady likes to keep her secrets. Besides, we don't have time now. We need to see a witch doctor about a corpse."

Okay, fine. Maybe you might not like spending your Saturday morning talking murder in a morgue with a vampire, but at that moment I was so happy I could have kissed Frank Reynolds for getting whacked with that hatchet.

Chapter 11

ON THE WALK TO THE building next door under an awning I suspected had been erected for Press's benefit, the vampire brought up a detail that had fallen through the cracks.

"Has Frank given you any idea why he thought Vanessa might also be in danger?"

Honestly, I'd completely forgotten that Frank had led with that concern when we met in the alley behind the shop—and after meeting Vanessa, I wasn't as inclined to worry about her as I should have been.

"He hasn't mentioned it again."

"Do you suppose he was talking about his brother?"

I'd gotten an unctuous, con artist, weasel vibe off Floyd, but he didn't read "murderer" on my personal character meter. "If he was," I said, "I think Frank would have said so at dinner last night. Being confronted with someone significant to their death typically cuts through afterlife amnesia for the recently departed."

"Maybe," Press said, "but Frank's a hard case in that department. I don't think he was all that bright to start with and that hatchet didn't help."

Unkind though it might have been, I agreed. "Frank will show up at some point today. I'll see what I can find out."

"How do you know he'll show up?"

"Because so far Uncle Grim and I are the only ones who can see and hear him. A guy who loves to talk as much as Frank does will ultimately come back to his only audience."

"Good point."

We found Santos wearing a lab coat and staring into the eyepiece of a microscope. In his own domain, the good doctor doesn't bother hiding his toothy bling or the tools of his trade.

Grotesque tribal masks adorned the walls alongside a collection of rattles and fetishes under a forest of medicine pouches dangling from the ceiling.

Santos heard us come in, but he continued studying the slide on his scope. "I don't have much to share with you. Frank Reynolds was in great health other than the head wound."

"Did you look at the back of his neck?" Press asked.

Santos was sitting on a wheeled stool. He pushed off with one foot and rolled in front of a computer. Punching a few keys, he called up a photo of Frank's neck. A series of scratches criss-crossed the pale skin.

"Well," Press said, "that explains why Frank said his neck itched. What did that?"

Santos shrugged. "No idea. I swabbed the marks and looked for residue, but came up empty."

"Did you do your witch doctor, woo-woo thing?" Press held out his hand and wobbled the fingers in mid-air to punctuate the question.

Santos scowled. "Yes, you bloodsucking bigot. I went into a trance and scanned for residual energy."

"And?"

"Whatever made the scratches was alive, and it wasn't an insect."

While the two of them had been bickering like the work couple they are, I took out my phone. Dragging a single image out of the diagram, I suspended the picture in the air to the left of the computer screen. "Did the same living, non-insect something make these scratches?"

Santos studied the two photographs. "Possibly."

Gesturing at the screen, I said, "Can I get a copy of that photo?"

Jerking a thumb toward the vampire, Santos said, "Don't ask me. It's his call."

Press shifted his weight and looked uncomfortable. Letting me into the inner circle and telling *other people* he'd let me in were two different things. Then, steeling himself, the vampire said in the most nonchalant tone he could manage, "Mattie is on the team now."

The witch doctor blinked a couple of times before busting into a toothy grin. "Congrats! You finally wore him down."

As the witch doctor and I exchanged a high five, Press growled, "Knock if off, Santos, or I'll boil you in your own iron pot."

"Play nice, boys," I warned as I copied the autopsy photo the easy way; I took a picture of the screen.

When I had what I needed, I brought up the next item on my list. "Let's talk about the vic's shoes."

"Loafers," Santos replied. "Probably his favorites. They've been re-soled at least once."

This time I accessed the photo of the purple stain. "What do you make of this? Did Reynolds step in something?"

Santos studied the image carefully, his expression growing thoughtful. "Man, I gotta lay off the peyote. I can't believe I missed that. It's not a stain; it's a drip."

As much as I wanted to ask the witch doctor about his use of hallucinogenic roots, I refrained because Santos was still talking.

"When I examined the head wound, the angle of the blow made me think the killer might have hesitated," he said, opening more autopsy photos on the computer screen. "But this drop mark could suggest the hatchet glanced off something before the blade went into the vic's skull."

Now interested, Press said, "Like whatever scratched up his neck?"

"Let's not jump to conclusions," Santos cautioned. "First I need to test the substance to see if it's blood."

Test the substance? "Santos," I said, "there can't be that many species with purple blood."

"Define 'that many,'" he replied. "I can list 3 or 4 dozen off the top of my head. I'll get back to you two when I have something definitive."

With that, he rolled back to his microscope, more or less dismissing us.

Press walked me to the lobby, but stopped short of the front door. "Sorry," he said. "End of the line for me. I left my shades in my office."

"That's fine," I assured him. "See you out at the Jones's tonight?"

"I wouldn't miss it—or our dance."

That response sent me skipping down the front steps to the Dodge. The instant I got behind the wheel, Frank materialized in the passenger seat.

"Well," I said, starting the car. "It's about time you showed up. I've got some questions for you, buddy."

The ghost looked offended. "Is that any way to speak to the victim of a recent fatal trauma?"

Ignoring the self-pitying whining, I said, "What have Vanessa and Floyd been up to since last night?"

"Not what I was afraid of," he admitted. "They slept in their own rooms and had breakfast together this morning. Vanessa has an appointment to get her hair done in an hour at some place called Bypassed Beauty."

I couldn't wait to share that one with Raylene. "By*gone* Beauty," I corrected, steering us past the courthouse heading toward the clock shop. "By the way, how did you and Vanessa meet, anyway?"

"At my weekly chess club."

I almost swerved into the cars parked on Main Street. "*Vanessa* belongs to a chess club?"

"No," Frank said, staring out the window like a tourist, "at the modeling agency next door. We just kept running into each other by accident day after day after day."

Uh huh.

He kept talking, sounding wistful. "We had so much in common. It was love at first sight."

Oh. This should be good. "What exactly did you have in common?"

"Everything," he said, sounding like a lovestruck puppy. "No matter what I brought up, she liked it, too." He paused and frowned like thinking hurt. "Her tastes certainly changed after we got married though."

I'll bet they did. Since the ghost was on a roll, I decided to risk tossing in a quick, out-of-context question in the hope that Frank would answer on reflex. "What does your business import?"

"Expensive things," he said without hesitating.

"What do you do with those things?"

"Make them more expensive."

Well. That was certainly a concise explanation of capitalism and inflation in four words. "Were you planning on making something more expensive here in Miller's Cove?"

Finally catching up to my strategy, Frank said, "You mean did I come to town to make a sale?"

"Exactly," I said as I pulled into my parking spot behind the shop. I cut the engine and turned to face the ghost. "Was this a business trip?"

He looked uncertain and flickered. "Maybe."

I wanted to ask if he really left the room the night of his death to meet someone, but I was afraid I'd lose him altogether. "Never mind. We can talk about that later. Come on inside with me. I need to check on my uncle."

The poor slob gave me an imploring look that actually did tug at my heartstrings, especially when he tacked on the world's most pathetic question. "When we're done can we go to the Bypassed Beauty and watch Vanessa get her hair done?"

"By*gone*, and I wouldn't miss it for the world."

Don't be so quick to judge. I meant what I said. Raylene's manicurist, Imogene, is Alma Abbott's sister and also a truth demon.

She might be able to get invaluable information out of Vanessa for me if I sweetened the deal and offered to perform a witchy favor in exchange.

As it happened, the Fates tossed me an even more interesting opportunity to gather information first.

When Frank and I went in the shop's back door, I looked toward the front only to see Uncle Grim waiting on Frank Reynolds. If you think the plot is about to thicken, you're right.

Chapter 12

IF UNCLE GRIM HEARD the back door, he didn't react, a sure sign that the deal at hand involved serious change. You have to understand that in Miller's Cove we deal in old things, some of which are highly collectible and thus valuable. Daddy made a wise choice when he steered the family into horology. There are months when the sale of a single timepiece puts the store into the profit column.

Other merchants could share similar scenarios with the wares they purvey. Consequently, even in a community dedicated to the concept of the "throwback," good security and insurance policies matter. There are high definition digital cameras hidden in the showroom ceiling that feed into a monitor in the back. Technically the devices are there to target shoplifters, but they're also tailor made for covert surveillance.

I went to the screen and zoomed in on the watch Grim had removed from the display case. The timepiece lay on a tray lined with soft black velvet perfectly aligned with the camera lens. I'd tell you that Floyd Reynolds had good taste, but he was shopping the price tags more than the watches.

His first pick was a 1918 Rolex officer's trench watch—925 sterling silver, 15 jewels, hand winding, and fully signed. It ticked off every box on a collector's list for desirable items. Uncle Grim earned his certification as a certified Rolex specialist before I was born. He picked the piece up on eBay for $2700. Fully cleaned and restored, we were asking $3500.

As Frank and I listened in, Floyd said, "Okay, this one is nice, but let's keep looking. What else can you show me? Kick up the price."

Grim reached into the case and brought out a second, more expensive Rolex—a Prince Doctor's watch with a two-tone 9k gold case made in the 1930s. It carried an asking price of $6295.

Looking back and forth between the two vintage watches, Floyd said, "Oh, what the heck. I'll take them both."

I thought Frank was going to blow up like he'd been hit with a *Ghostbusters* proton beam. The guy might have post-mortem amnesia, but his grade school memories for basic addition were in perfect shape. "Where is a bum like Floyd going to come up with $9795 before taxes?"

"Apparently from his pocket," I answered, pointing at the video screen.

The living Reynolds brother took a slim wallet out of the breast pocket of his gangster pinstripe suit and proceeded to peel off twenty $500 bills, which Uncle Grim refused to accept.

Before you decide my uncle suffers from early onset dementia, he couldn't accept those portraits of William McKinley because his ethics wouldn't let him. While I explain why, keep an image of Floyd Reynolds throwing a fit in the forefront of your mind. He ranted and raved for a good five minutes while Uncle Grim listened with his trademark unflappable patience.

The United States stopped printing the $500 bill in 1945 and discontinued the denomination entirely in 1969. The bills are still legal tender, but they're worth a heck of a lot more to collectors—up to 40% more than their stated face value.

The paper money Floyd put down on the counter was so crisp the bills might very well have been uncirculated, which meant they could command a premium price.

I didn't have all the figures in front of me at the time, but working some rapid fire mental math, I estimated that Floyd was trying to spend $9795 with collectible paper money worth at least $12,000.

Beside me, Frank swore under his breath and said, "They closed the deal. They're supposed to be mourning me and they closed the deal. It's bad enough to be murdered, but to be betrayed like this? It's unbearable."

Detouring past sympathy and taking the direct route to sleuthing, I said, "Closed the deal on what, Frank? Come on. Remember. This is important."

"I can't remember," he said, growing more agitated by the second, "but I'm telling you this is grave robbing."

Frank's body was lying on a stainless steel shelf in Santos's morgue, so no graves were yet involved in the commission of this crime, but I took his meaning.

Our chance witnessing of the aborted Rolex buy added new questions to my working case diagram. What item or items did Frank bring to Miller's Cove that were worth at least $12,000? And who in town would pay for said item or items in valuable, discontinued, mint-condition currency?

The presence of the $500 bills certainly fit the town's anachronistic theme right down to the 1945 cut off date, but who kept that kind of cash on hand?

The furious clanging of the bell on the shop door returned my attention to the present situation. Grim appeared in the workroom door and said, "You catch all that?"

"We did."

"First time I've ever had a customer give me a piece of his mind and storm out when I tried to *save* him money."

Frank was so upset by that time he was flashing like a cheap disco ball. "You saved *my* money, not *his*. Money which that traitorous twin brother of mine shouldn't have. Just like he shouldn't have my wife."

Keeping one ear on Frank, who was just warming up to a proper tirade, I drew Uncle Grim aside. "I guess you noticed the resemblance to my client?"

"The minute the other one walked in the door. That money is burning a hole in the living one's pocket."

"Floyd," I supplied.

"Well, whoever he is, that guy cares more about buying something—*anything*—than losing money paying for it with collectible bills."

The predictable behavior of someone who just came into a large sum. "About the vintage cash," I said. "Any idea who in town might be sitting on that much out-of-date folding money?"

Grim rubbed at his jaw. "Well, when it comes to money, I always say look to the leprechauns first, but those boys lean more toward gold."

"True, but William McKinley was the descendant of an Irish farmer."

My uncle was impressed at my command of useless, esoteric history. "How do you know that?"

"Trivia night at the Deja Vu. Raylene and I are the reigning champs."

Grim looked hurt. "And you didn't invite me?"

"Sorry. The tournaments are the same night as your lodge meeting. We were discussing leprechauns?"

"Oh, right. In my experience the little guys are too preoccupied with beard maintenance and shamrocks to read much history."

"Any other likely suspects?"

Looking over my shoulder, Grim said, "Can you ask him to stop that?"

Following my uncle's line of sight, I saw Frank pacing back and forth through the middle of Grim's workbench. Nobody, ectoplasmic or not, is allowed to touch that workspace.

"Frank," I called out. "Watch the furniture."

The ghost ignored me and continued basically frothing at the mouth. "And to *think* I was worried about that woman! I only stayed down here with the living because I thought the buyer would come after her when I lost them."

"Frank!"

The spirit stopped pacing, halting mid-bench with Grim's work light protruding from his chest—which looked oddly symmetrical against the hatchet in the back of his head. "Would you please stop yelling at me? If I'd had any idea haunting would be this stressful, I never would have taken it on."

"I'll make sure the mortician puts Valium in the embalming fluid," I snapped. "Who was the buyer and what did you lose?"

Frank looked like he was on the verge of tears. "My life. I lost my life. And then I lost my wife. Or maybe I'd already lost her. Who cares about the deal when I'm like this and Floyd gets everything that was mine? I know life isn't fair, but isn't death supposed to be the great equalizer? Because I'm not feeling equal, that's for darn sure."

Beside me, Grim clucked his tongue. "Blade went in deep, didn't it?"

"You have no idea," I replied. "Did Floyd say where he was going when you wouldn't take his money?"

"No, but he did allow as how he was killing time while his sister-in-law got her hair done."

"Well, she's supposed to be at Raylene's in twenty minutes, so I guess that's where we're going."

My uncle nodded. "Good enough. I'll ask the boys about the $500 bills and get back to you."

"The boys" are my uncle's closest cronies. They're all about the same age, all skilled craftsmen, and either old bachelors like Grim or widowers. The group eats supper together several times a week at the Guild Hall outside of town well away from the prying presence of the tourists.

The Guild Hall is a hangover from the craftsmen's guilds of Medieval Europe. The Miller's Cove version occupies that place where a VFW hall meets a secret lodge with arcane symbols and handshakes. Come to think of it, the boys belong to one of those, too.

Anyway, people can only gain Guild Hall membership by invitation, and I haven't been invited. I do, however, have access to the group's bottomless well of information—also known as gossip—through Uncle Grim.

If anybody in Miller's Cove could get me a lead on those $500 bills it would be the Guild members. For now, I had to get Frank calmed down so we could go watch Vanessa get her hair done and hopefully sing like a canary in the process.

Chapter 13

THIS TIME I LEFT THE Dodge behind the shop and walked through the alley to Bygone Beauty. Period detail extends behind the scenes—and buildings—in Miller's Cove. You won't find any garbage trucks with articulated retrieval arms around here.

Frank and I passed battered silver trash cans with lids that begged to be ripped off and used as shields in a child's fantasy battle. Patches of weeds and vines snaked around gas and electrical meters, attaching themselves to cast-off signs and broken furniture before climbing the nearest vertical surface.

Kids can no more resist hidden and abandoned places than they can say no to candy, so it didn't surprise me when I heard bike tires in the gravel behind us.

Two young boys and a girl in overalls and pigtails braked and let loose with a chorus of, "Hi, Miss Tuckers!"

The trio—Bobby Tompkins, Kenny Elliott, and Linda Sue Finley—are a common sight around town on summer days and when school is out. Unlike most kids in the outside, modern world, this trio relies on the magical elixir of bikes, hide outs, and imagination to entertain themselves.

"Hey, you all," I greeted them. "What are you up to?"

Linda Sue answered. "We're going to the matinee at the Memory Palace."

"What's playing?"

"*The Thief of Bagdad*," Kenny said in an excited voice. "The genie looks swell and there's a flying carpet."

Bobby chimed in. "It's a double feature. Red Ryder's the second picture, *Murder on the Santa Fe Trail.*"

"Well, you all have fun," I said. "Be careful crossing Main Street."

That last bit made me cringe. Sometimes I sound more like my mother than I care to admit.

The kids pushed off amid a cloud of dust and "yes, ma'ams." Frank watched them pedal away. He looked like he wanted to go to the picture show, too.

"They aren't acting, are they?" he said.

"Excuse me?"

"When I read the brochure for this place I thought you'd all be actors, but you really do live in the past."

"Well, our version of it."

The ghost's outline sharpened, which I took as an effort on his part to focus. "But you aren't just people like the rest of us."

Even though I was speaking to a man in no position to give away town secrets, I became reflexively evasive. "What do you mean?"

Frank frowned. "None of you are ordinary. You're all different somehow and I think maybe some of you have powers or something. It's okay, I won't tell anyone. I'm right, aren't I?"

Taking pity on the guy, I said, "Yes, you're right."

The spirit's moment of clarity departed as quickly as it had arrived. In a far off voice, he mumbled, "I thought he was dumb, but he really didn't know."

I suspected Frank was talking about the mystery buyer again, but I needed my client to remain present and stable during Vanessa's hair appointment. I'd been covertly using transcription magic to record Frank's disjointed revelations before adding them to the working case file on my phone.

Although he had no awareness of doing so, the ghost was supplying random but useful bread crumbs that could reveal the motive behind his death, and maybe even the identity of the killer. I hoped seeing

Vanessa would trigger more of the quasi-clues, which had been steadily increasing in number as Frank got used to functioning on the other side.

Channeling my inner border collie, I herded Frank through the backdoor of the salon, which coincidentally was the same moment Vanessa sashayed in the front door.

Granted everyone does grief their own way, but donning widow's weeds didn't seem to be in Vanessa's action plan. She wore a fuchsia pencil skirt plastered to her hips in a fit so snug I swear I heard her internal organs begging for mercy.

Without a millimeter of tucking space, she'd opted for a long white satin blouse with a fitted waist, which she'd belted. The effect put her forward facing assets on sculpted display.

To be honest, the woman looked like a gun moll for a low-rent mob boss.

Beside me, Frank gasped, "Isn't she gorgeous?"

He didn't hear the noncommittal noise I made in response. In a flash the ghost left me like a piece of yesterday's liver in favor of hovering around Vanessa. If he'd had functioning salivary glands, we'd have had a drool emergency on aisle one.

As Raylene checked Vanessa in, my friend caught sight of me over the double swinging doors that separate the back room from the salon proper. I put a finger to my lips and shook my head.

Acknowledging my request for discretion with a wink, Raylene led Vanessa over to a stylist with Frank in invisible tow.

Vanessa couldn't see her ardent admirer, but the hairdresser frowned and stared hard in the ghost's direction before shaking out the plastic cape and saying, "What are we doing, honey?"

"I've just had the *worst* couple of days," Vanessa lamented. "I need a new do to cheer me up and we're going to the Copycat Club tonight, so make me look like that woman from the movie."

She meant Ingrid Bergman in *Casablanca*. Apparently Vanessa and Floyd planned a night on the town.

Raylene took her time coming to the back to avoid directing anyone's attention toward me. She stopped to chat with clients and to confer with the operators, offering compliments and words of aesthetic advice.

Like her staff, Raylene wore a white smock with intertwined gold "B's" appliquéd on the left shoulder. The style mirrored the cream and gold decor of the establishment.

A line of women sat under the permanent wave machines. With the descending mass of cords attached to their hair, they looked like the victims of a massed octopus attack.

When Raylene finally came through the double doors, she pointed toward her office. I nodded and followed her inside. She closed the door and gestured at the air around us. "Do we have company?"

"No. Frank's out there watching Vanessa get her hair done."

"Well," Raylene said, sitting in her high-backed desk chair, "he's hard up for entertainment. Is there a plan involved in this visit or are we winging it?"

"There's a plan. You're going to comp Vanessa a manicure."

Raylene arched one perfectly plucked brow. "Oh, a plan that cuts into my profit margin. I love it."

Smiling weakly, I said, "Lunch is on me next time."

"Let me guess. You want to bribe Imogene to pump Vanessa while we listen."

I couldn't get that lucky twice in one day. "We can't listen in. You don't have security cameras."

"No," she agreed, "I have something better—Aqua Netta."

She meant a vintage 1940s glamor girl head vase that had been with Raylene since beauty school. The glazed ceramic piece, named for the south's signature hairspray, depicted a blond woman with a blue hair bow coyly looking over one shoulder.

From her penciled on eyebrows and fake eyelashes to the crimson bow mouth, Aqua Netta epitomized kitsch. When Raylene found the "treasure" in a second-hand shop it came with a surveillance spell taped to the base.

We'd awakened Aqua Netta one time, entirely forgetting that we didn't know how to put her back to sleep. For six hours we had to deal with an animate vase with a thick Brooklyn accent and zero filter.

"We are *not* using Aqua Netta," I said firmly. "She's worse than one of those black velvet Elvis paintings. Her eyes follow you everywhere."

Fidgeting and smoothing her hair—which didn't need to be smoothed—Raylene said, "I've been working with her. She knows not to do that now."

My mouth dropped open. "You've been waking Aqua Netta up without me?"

"Well, now, sugar," Raylene hedged. "You said it yourself. She makes you nervous."

"Don't you 'now sugar' me," I said. "Besides, I'm not sure I trust Aqua Netta to give us an accurate account of whatever Vanessa says."

Lifting an over-sized handheld mirror from the shelf behind her, Raylene slipped on a pair of rhinestone bedazzled reading glasses. "She won't have to say a word. Watch and don't judge."

With that, she took a yellowed index card out of the top desk drawer. Tape residue marked the corners. Clearing her throat, Raylene read:

Eyes of blue for to see,
Ears alive for to hear,
Awaken now and bring to me,
That which lies before thee.

"That is *not* the original spell," I accused.

"I told you I've been working on it, now hush!"

A pinpoint formed in the center of the mirror. As it expanded, we saw the interior of the salon over a row of nail polish bottles. The view afforded us a good angle of Vanessa, her hair done up on one side in oversized curlers.

Raylene clucked her tongue. "I told Betty not to use those big rollers. Ingrid's hair didn't have that much bounce in *Casablanca*."

Ignoring the coiffure critique, I said, "Aqua Netta is on the shelf behind Imogene's table?"

"Yes, and she understands that people get creeped out if she moves her eyes. Really, give her a chance. She's good at this."

Still suspicious, I asked, "What's in this arrangement for Aqua Netta?"

"Movies. Every time I wake her up, she gets a trip to the Palace."

I couldn't believe what I was hearing. "Raylene, why are you spying on your customers?"

She looked at me like I needed my roots done. "Sugar, a woman in my line of work has to know everything, and I do mean *everything* that goes on in this town."

"And you employ a truth demon for a manicurist in full sight of an enchanted vase. It's an efficient set up. I'll give you that, but I can't believe you've been holding out on me."

Turning serious, Raylene said, "I'm sorry, Mattie. Let me and Aqua Netta make it up to you. If anyone can get Vanessa to slip up and talk, it's Imogene."

"Well, fine," I said in a fake huff. "But I'm going to the *Palace* with you and Aqua Netta and *you're* buying me the big popcorn bucket."

"Done!" Raylene said, slipping the mirror in a base clearly designed for that purpose. "I'll be right back."

She returned in the company of a short woman with a voice like sandpaper and wiry, short curls to match. Imogene's froggish features broke into a grin when she saw me—a grin that only expanded when I explained what I wanted her to do.

At my offer for a magical favor in return, Imogene said, "That'll take some thinking. I don't want to waste a free spell. Can you give me a raincheck?"

"Absolutely."

"Okay then," she said, standing and clapping her hands. "Fasten your seatbelts, girls. Me and Aqua Netta are on the case."

Chapter 14

RAYLENE GAVE IMOGENE enough time to get settled at her table before going out to talk with Vanessa. I watched everything through Aqua Netta's eyes—literally.

In Raylene's place I would have come out of the gate with sympathy in the lead, but she put her money on Vanessa's vanity. After all, vanity keeps Raylene's business afloat. That's one emotion she knows inside out.

"Mrs. Reynolds, you are the *living image* of Ingrid Bergman."

Frank, still hovering at his wife's elbow, looked ready to burst with pride.

Vanessa heard the words, but they fell on a barren ground of incomprehension, which moved the stylist to help out. "She means that woman from the movie."

A light bulb went on over Vanessa's head—granted one of low wattage, but a bulb all the same. "*Thank you!* We bought a white suit for Frank to wear like the club owner Bogart guy in the picture. It fits Floyd, so we didn't lose a thing."

That response hit Frank hard. An unhealthy shimmer passed through the spirit that only deepened my worry. His upset of the day before had been replaced first by bewilderment and now renewed Vanessa worship.

Mental breakdowns aren't exclusively for the living. There are plenty of things to make a person go off the rails on either side of the veil. Most ghosts make steady progress coping with their situation, but Frank seemed to be regressing. If he became too unstable, he might not be able to cross over at all.

Vanessa's clueless reply about the white suit even made Raylene take a beat. The wife and brother were absolutely guilty of insensitivity and bad taste, but more and more I suspected them of worse transgressions.

When Raylene finally did speak, the way she drew out the words told me she'd really like to say, *"Lady, you are some piece of work,"* but with more colorful adjectives.

Instead, she said, "Well, that's really good, but honey you can't go to the Copycat Club wearing that shade of nail polish. It's not the color Ingrid wore in the movie.

Vanessa frowned, "Wasn't that a black and white picture?"

"It was, but the Copycat is in color and that's where you're going to be. Come on now. Let's get you all fixed up. On the house."

Brightening, Vanessa said, "Well, if it's free."

The salon door let out a subdued ding and Floyd entered the building. "You ready to go, Vanessa?" he asked, still sounding surly from his encounter with Uncle Grim.

"No," Vanessa said, "I still have to get my nails done. Did you buy yourself a new watch?"

Floyd's neck flushed bright red. "That shop carries a lot of outdated junk. I didn't find anything there or in any of the other stores I went into. I'll get a good watch when we get back home. Come on."

I'll admit I rankled at the insult to the clock shop and had the dark thought that Floyd better watch himself. I'm not above the stray hex in the defense of family honor.

Vanessa wouldn't budge. "Quit being a grumpy Gus. You can wait for me in the seating area. They have magazines."

Right, that 1942 copy of *Marie-Claire* had Floyd's name written all over it.

"Fine," he grumbled. "I need to make some calls anyway."

Raylene shut that down before the jerk's cell phone cleared his breast pocket.

"I am so sorry, sir. Miller's Cove has an ordinance outlawing the public use of undisguised cellular devices."

The red on Floyd's neck deepened to magenta. "You cannot be serious."

"I'm afraid I am. You can go across the street to the post office and use one of the pay phone booths if you like. The windows are opaque so no one will see you using technology that doesn't fit the town's stated time period."

Frank left, but not without a good bit of mouthing about a two-bit tourist trap carrying "the schtick" too far.

Vanessa took her seat across from Imogene. "Don't pay any attention to him. He's lactose intolerant. He forgot his pills and we can't get almond milk at the Lodge. They didn't have almonds in the 1940s. I think it was a war thing."

Raylene and Imogene exchanged a look, but didn't say anything. When Raylene came back, she juggled two coffee cups and had a box of Girl Scout cookies wedged under her elbow.

That's right. The Girl Scouts have been around since 1912. They started getting the nation addicted to those cookies in 1917.

Due to wartime shortages of sugar, flour, and butter, the girls switched to calendars in 1944, but the cookies returned in 1945. In Miller's Cove, we pretend that lone cookie-less year never happened.

At the sight of the box, I realized I was ravenous. Those eggs and that piece of toast had been hours ago and a lot had happened since. "Let's hit the Deja Vu when Imogene finishes with Vanessa. I'm starved."

"Good idea," Raylene agreed, positioning the mirror so we could both see the action. "You can catch me up on your meeting with Press this morning."

When I broke into a smile, Raylene said, "*Ooooh!* It went that well?"

I nodded. "I'll tell you all about it later. Imogene's getting started."

While we'd been talking, the manicurist confirmed Vanessa did not have acrylic nails, removed her existing polish with acetone-soaked cotton balls, and started to shape her nails.

"So," Imogene said, "was that man your husband?"

"Oh, no," Vanessa said. "Floyd is my brother-in-law. His twin brother, Frank, is...er...*was* my husband. He's dead now."

"I'm so sorry. Did he die suddenly?"

"He went to get ice and someone hit him on the head with a hatchet."

Imogene, like every other Miller's Cove resident, knew exactly what happened at the Nostalgia Nook, but she faked a shocked reaction like a pro. "How horrible for you!"

"I think it was probably worse for him. I'm sorry he's dead, but really, I married the wrong brother." She stopped as confusion washed over her face. "Why did I say that?"

Because she was holding hands with a truth demon.

"Don't you worry about a thing," Imogene soothed. "We're just having us some girl talk. What was your husband like?"

Frank appeared beside me so suddenly I almost spilled my coffee. "Stop this!" he demanded "I don't want to hear what she says."

Helping me steady my cup, Raylene said, "Frank?"

"Yes. He doesn't want to hear his wife talk about him."

Through the mirror, Vanessa said, "Frank knew about lots of things, and he was good at making money. Life is a lot easier when somebody makes money you can spend, but I didn't know about Floyd until Frank and I were already married."

"Of course she didn't know," Frank said with anguish. "Because Floyd ruins everything and I didn't want her to know. I've heard enough. I'm out of here."

The agitated spirit blipped out before I could even attempt to calm him down.

"He's gone again," I told Raylene. "I'm genuinely concerned about the poor man. I don't want Frank to get stuck down here."

"*Shhhh!*" Raylene hissed. "Listen."

"Floyd just has so much more charisma," Vanessa was saying. "He takes risks and does exciting things. Frank belonged to a chess club."

"Did the brothers get along?" Imogene asked, now applying the new polish.

"Not really. They were very competitive. Floyd wasn't always nice to Frank."

By that time, Vanessa's voice sounded dreamy and detached. Imogene had lulled her into a trance-like, cooperative state.

"Was he not nice enough to kill his brother?" Imogene prodded gently

"Not on purpose," Vanessa replied. She looked like she wanted to say more, but Frank came back into the salon and interrupted the session.

"We really have to get back to the Lodge, Vanessa. I've had all the small town retro bull I can take. I got inside one of those stupid phone booths and only had one bar on my phone. One stinking bar. What the heck am I supposed to do with that? Besides, you said you wanted time to watch that movie again."

Apparently Vanessa planned to hone her Bergman impression, hopefully starting by learning the woman's name.

"She's all done," Imogene said. "Just let her stay under the drying light for a minute or two."

Vanessa looked at Imogene with the dazed expression of a person awakening from a deep sleep. "That was the most relaxing manicure I've ever had."

Over her shoulder, Floyd looked straight into Aqua Netta's eyes. "*That*," he said, pointing toward the shelf, "is the ugliest vase I've ever seen."

"Don't let the owner hear you say that," Imogene warned. "That vase is a rare collectible."

"Huh," Floyd said. "Just goes to show expensive stuff can look like total crap." He glanced down to say something to Vanessa, but his head snapped right back up. "That thing blinked."

Imogene trilled out a dismissive laugh. "People say that all the time. It's the glaze over the paint. Creates an optical illusion."

Floyd didn't look convinced. "This town is weird as hell." With that, he threw a $20 bill on the table as a tip. "Come on, Vanessa. I'm starting to get really creeped out by all this make-believe time travel."

Vanessa allowed herself to be led out and Raylene reversed the incantation before Aqua Netta could react overtly to Floyd's insults.

"She's going to give us an ear full over that 'ugliest vase' crack when we take her to movie night," Raylene warned.

"I don't blame her," I said. "That was rude. What do you suppose Vanessa meant when she said Floyd wouldn't kill Frank on purpose?"

Raylene paused at the door. "That he killed his brother by accident?"

I'd already tried to jump to the same conclusion, but stumbled over a logical hurdle. How, exactly, does a guy ax someone in the head by accident?

Chapter 15

"HEY, YOU TWO," ROSIE said as she put glasses of iced tea we didn't order in front of us along with a basket of rolls. "I put a couple of meat loaf plates back just in case. You all good with that?"

Already slathering butter on one of the rolls, I said, "Bless you, Rosie. I'm so hungry I could eat a horse."

"No horse on the menu until Thursday, but come back Tuesday for the mule." She winked and bustled off to get our food.

"I hope she doesn't talk like that to the tourists," Raylene said, adding sugar to her tea. "If Vanessa Reynolds is any gauge, they'll believe Rosie does a mean jackass fricassee."

"*Mmmmmm*," I said, chewing my roll. "Donkey stew. My favorite. Talking about feeding mystery meat to the tourists, since when does Miller's Cove have an undisguised public cell phone ordinance?"

"Since never, but it got Floyd out of the shop so we didn't have to listen to him."

Our plates arrived and we both tucked in like we hadn't eaten in days. Rosie's meatloaf is a local institution. Blindfolded you'd swear that was sirloin on your fork.

I polished off my meal so fast Rosie asked me if I had a tapeworm before replacing my empty plate with a full one.

"You're a lifesaver, Rosie."

"No starvation allowed in my hash joint," she said. "Be right back with pie and coffee."

Raylene watched me shoveling meatloaf and mashed potatoes. "*Do you have a tapeworm?*"

"Sorry," I said, wiping my mouth. "Full morning. Keeping that transcription spell running around Frank is exhausting especially since I never know when he's going to show up. Some of those vague statements of his could be clues."

"You're excused," Raylene said, accepting a mug of coffee and a slice of apple pie from Rosie. Regulars at the Deja Vu enjoy special privileges. Raylene and I are such permanent fixtures, we get the family treatment.

"I hope you don't need this table," Raylene said. "Mattie won't be able to move for at least an hour. I won't be surprised if she stretches out for a nap."

"Table's always yours and if Mattie needs a nap, she should go right ahead and take one. You all stay as long as you like."

Pushing the plate away, I said, "You can take this, Rosie. I'm slowing down.

When we were alone again, Raylene dictated our opening topic. "Okay. Now. First things first. Press."

"He invited me to officially join the investigation."

Raylene choked so hard on her coffee I had to get up and pound her on the back. When she could breathe again, she ordered me to, "Sit. Start over. Leave *nothing* out."

Replaying my conversation with Press for Raylene's benefit brought back the tingle of excitement I feel when I'm with the vampire. Some people might assure you that sensation signals an impending involuntary blood donation, but I never worry about my personal safety with Press. If anything, he's the one in danger—from me.

Ultimately my recap brought me and Raylene back to the murder at hand.

"I know you can't show me your case board in public," Raylene said, "so run it down for me."

Normally we'd go through this exercise in my den over wine and an indoor picnic, but by mutual agreement we would be working with a tight timeline for the remainder of that Saturday.

Raylene agreed to join me at the Jones' place and then be present for a late night rendezvous with the ghost of a moonshiner named Shifty at the Nostalgia Nook. Be patient. I'll get to that part.

In anticipation of this conversation, I'd worked out my laundry list of troubling facts, starting with Floyd and Vanessa having an affair. That relationship pointed to a quick and easy solution to the crime, which I didn't buy.

Neither did Raylene. "Too cut and dried. The brother's a jerk, but he doesn't strike me as a murderer."

"Santos says Frank's head wound indicates his assailant either hesitated or hit something else first."

"Like what?"

"Maybe whatever scratched up Frank's neck and left a purple stain on his shoe sole."

"Didn't you see scratches in the hotel room, too?"

"Yep. Same pattern."

"So what are you thinking? Some bug jumped on Frank's neck and went to the ice machine with him and then Frank managed to step on the little guy?"

That could be the scenario, or there could have been more than one of whatever made the scratches. Frowning, I said, "Do bugs bleed purple? For that matter, do bugs *have* blood at all?"

Raylene took out her phone, sticking her tongue out at me when I mentioned that the device wasn't legally disguised.

After some hunting and pecking with her index finger, she said, "Bug blood has hemolympha heterogeneous fluid, but no red blood cells."

"Meaning?"

"If a squashed bug caused that stain, the mark would be yellow or green. *Oh!* Here's a cool fact."

Juggling dread and curiosity, I said, "I'm afraid to ask, but tell me."

"You know that red you see when you smack a fly? It's from the pigment in their eyes."

Good thing I have a strong stomach. "So, not a mystery purple-blooded creepy crawly. In some ways, I feel better."

"Me, too," Raylene said, signaling Rosie to refill our cups. Since we were likely to be up most of the night, I didn't worry about overloading on caffeine.

Refortified with fresh Joe, we resumed our review of the known facts.

"The suggestion of hesitation does interest me," I said. "Especially after Vanessa's remark that Floyd wouldn't kill Frank on purpose."

"True, but aren't there witnesses who can confirm Floyd's arrival at the Lodge *after* the body was discovered?"

"Yes, and Floyd doesn't look like someone who travels with an ax."

Blowing on the hot liquid in her cup before taking a sip, Raylene asked, "Is he driving his personal vehicle or a rental car?"

"I don't know. Why?"

"Because some people carry survival stuff in their trunks. I suppose that could include a hatchet."

Making a note to run down that detail, we went over the missing ice scoop and bucket as well as the odd position of the corpse. Which is when I told Raylene about my plan to call in Shifty.

In life the man's nickname derived from his dedication to various nefarious means of earning a living. Those wrong-side-of-the-law occupations included moonshining. Since his death, Shifty has worked for me on multiple occasions in exchange for a "charge up."

Although I can't say I wield the skill with any real degree of accuracy, I can still use my EMF to juice a ghost to near corporeality for a brief period—typically around five minutes. Coincidentally, that's exactly how much time Shifty needs to enjoy a hefty nip of the product he used to distill.

In exchange, Shifty investigates tight spaces for me—like the drain underneath the ice machine.

I explained to Raylene that I planned for us to hit the Lodge after we left the Jones land which would be in the wee hours of the morning.

Getting her onboard required no convincing. "Call me Mata Hari," she said with enthusiasm. "Up for any mission."

"Mata Hari was a spy, not a detective."

Facts typically don't faze Raylene. "Spy. Detective. Whatever. All I know is that Garbo played the socks off the woman in 1931 and Adrian did the gowns for the picture."

Searching my memory, I said, "Didn't the Hays Office censor that movie in 1934?"

"Oh, Lord yes. I imagine most of them were reaching for their nitroglycerin tablets before the end of the first reel."

"Why?"

"Too many scenes that required no wardrobe at all, if you follow my drift."

I did follow, and could well imagine the reaction of the Hayes office, the censorship entity under which the Hollywood studios functioned from 1930 to 1966. The strict production code wouldn't even allow married couples to be filmed in the same bed.

Garbo may well have left acting because she wanted to be alone, but she was also fed up with the prudes.

"What do you expect Shifty to find down the drain pipe?" Raylene asked.

"I don't know, but I believe Frank came to Miller's Cove to sell something to a local who agreed to pay in uncirculated $500 bills without realizing their true value. Uncle Grim plans to run that by the boys at the Guild Hall."

Since Raylene needed to get back to Bygone Beauty and I had to go see Shifty, I gave her an abbreviated summary of the credit card situation at the Lodge.

"That's all I know so far. Press suggested I talk to Remi myself at the Jones' place, so you'll be there for that conversation."

Raylene had grown solemn while I talked. "I don't like the part about Buckshot telling Press to stand down. It would break my heart to find out the mayor's up to something shady."

Her reaction mirrored my feelings. Buckshot not only engineered the Miller's Cove transformation, he's one of our leading and most beloved citizens.

For instance, he recently came up with the idea to sell replica "war bonds" to the tourists with all proceeds going to charities in the human world. "They pay our bills," Buckshot explained. "It's only right we do something for them,"

Raylene and I sat in silence until she broke the tension with a critical question. "Have you thought about what you're going to wear? We should coordinate our look."

That angst-busting question alone should help you understand why I love Raylene. She always finds a way to shine light into the darkest hours.

"I'll probably put on another blouse and different shoes, but otherwise I'm going like this."

"Pick a dark color," she advised. "We'll need to be covert at the lodge."

In the company of a glowing moonshiner who likes to accessorize with a shotgun draped over one arm. No problem.

Chapter 16

AFTER PROMISING TO pick Raylene up around eight o'clock, I pointed the nose of the Dodge south and drove into the mountains. We are blessed to live in a beautiful place that keeps our hearts close to the animating force of nature and the land.

Rolling the window down and driving under the speed limit on the deserted secondary road, I let my mind continue to turn over the case details. At one point I even called out to Frank asking him to join me.

The ghost didn't answer, which came as no surprise. I doubted he could even hear me, but I had to try. The afterlife wasn't working out well for Frank Reynolds. His plight tugged at my heart.

Sure, I take these jobs to make a living, but I always wind up caring about my clients. Frank might have been a confused mess, but he was my responsibility and I hated to think that he felt alone.

Anytime I work with a ghost, I try to put myself in their position both before and after death claimed them. That theory about the restless dead having unfinished business accurately describes their dilemma, but "unfinished business" covers a lot of territory.

Sometimes the deceased has a task to complete or critical information to pass on. In other instances, the dead require something from the living—like justice and closure as in Frank's case.

That doesn't seem like a lot to ask for when someone has gone and put an ax in your skull. I mean, really. Outside of books and movies, who does that?

The hardest spirits to help are those that have attached themselves to events that cannot be undone or righted.

Take spectral soldiers, as an example. There are multiple ghosts stuck at the Gettysburg battlefield in Pennsylvania. The land has the questionable distinction as the most haunted military site in the United States.

No one can change the conclusion of the horrific clash of armies during which they lost their lives nor can the outcome of the war itself be altered. Friends and brothers killed one another on that ground. Some died instantly, others lingered for hours, even days, in intense pain.

With that type of haunting the only approach involves the presentation of possibility. Those lost souls don't have to stay on the site of their suffering and death, but giving them that information rarely, if ever, works.

I do occasionally take a case purely to try to get a haunt to move on, but not often. The dead who are truly chained to some empty echo of their lives are just too sad. I didn't want that for Frank Reynolds.

After a 20 minute drive, I turned down a dirt road, stopped, laid a thick anti-ding barrier around the Dodge, and then headed for the foothills.

Parking in a clearing at the tree line, I got out and started to climb, counting the minutes until the first shotgun blast hit me.

Shifty disproves that old saw "you can't take it with you." He died during a running gun battle with the revenuers, but a bullet didn't take him out. Trying to kill those government men had him so preoccupied, Shifty failed to pay attention to his still—his very large still. When Boozy Betzy blew, she took out the whole camp and everything in it, which allowed Shifty to keep it all, including his double-barrel 20 gauge.

This ghost has an attachment to both a place and an event, but he's not unhappy about anything except his inability to take a drink.

Given how Shifty died, I can't blame him for shooting everyone who comes up his trail, but *dang* that ectoplasmic buckshot itches going through you.

Oh, and one more thing. I couldn't tell Press what I had in mind to move our investigation along. As a freshly turned vamp home from Chicago and determined to make a name for himself on the Miller's Cove police force, Press called in the revenuers who killed Shifty.

I came around a big boulder on the trail and took a load of shot full in the chest. "Hecate's *hair pins,* Shifty! Do you *have* to do that?"

A battered felt hat poked out of the bushes atop a mess of unruly, tangled hair. "Mattie girl? That you?"

"You're looking at me, aren't you?"

"Couldn't take a chance on you being one of J. Edgar's boys."

Scratching vigorously, I said, "I think you mean the Bureau of Alcohol, Tobacco, and Firearms."

A cackling laugh emanated from the underbrush. "Not during Prohibition, I don't. Something just ain't right about that J. Edgar Hoover."

Like a closet full of high heels, but we didn't have time for that discussion. A dead, East Tennessee moonshiner wasn't a candidate to become "woke."

Shifty came out from his hiding place with that old 20-gauge draped over one elbow. "Come on into camp, Mattie. I'd offer you a taste of shine, but thanks to that no count bloodsucking Yankee boy, I can't even drink my own liquor."

As I followed the ghost higher up the mountain, I defended Press from that completely unfair insult. "He is *not* a Yankee and you know it."

"That don't make no never mind," Shifty said with bitter conviction. "Living up north ruined that boy way more than being turned into an unholy critter of the night."

Shifty's father fought for the South, leaving his boy with entrenched prejudices toward the federal government and all things Northern. Arguing with the moonshiner would get me nowhere, plus I was trying not to laugh over the phrase "critter of the night." Imagine that wording on Dracula's business card.

Boozy Betsy, intact and functional on the other side, bubbled merrily over a blazing ghost fire. Shifty offered me one of the rickety wood folding chairs that would do me about as much good as sitting on thin air.

Instead, I chose a seat on a low rock and watched Shifty poke at the fire. "What brought you up the mountain, Mattie girl?" he finally asked.

"I have a job for you."

Shifty's form crackled with excited anticipation. "Thank the Good Lord! I am fair starved for a drink. What's the job?"

I hadn't been looking forward to this part. Keeping my voice light, I said, "Oh, nothing complicated. Just going down a drain pipe at the Nostalgia Nook Lodge."

The ghost made a disapproving face, showing me two rows of uneven, yellowed teeth before spitting a stream of eternal tobacco juice at the flames. "I ain't no two-bit plumber."

"Well," I said, "that's not strictly true. You built Betsy, didn't you? Isn't distilling liquor kind of like plumbing?"

Shifty looked like I'd insulted his Mama and his best coon dog at the same time. "This ole gal here is a work of pure art, not some goldurned Sears & Roebuck washing machine."

'Which is good, because the drain I want you to search is under an *ice* machine."

Moving the wad of tobacco from one cheek to the other, the ghost said, "Don't know nothing 'bought one of them neither. In my day we waited for winter to come on to get ice."

Most of Shifty's protests were all for show. I knew the spirit too well. He would have materialized inside a septic tank to get paid with enough corporeality to get a snort. I tried again.

"All you have to do is go down the pipe and look for anything interesting that might have fallen into the drain."

Eying me with open suspicion, he said, "Then what."

"You bring whatever it is up out of the pipe for me."

The ghost let out a stream of profanity and kicked at the dirt. "Lord have mercy and land of Goshen! I *knew* there was a catch, woman. That gosh darned grab-it magic turns me green for a solid month."

The one drawback to sending a ghost operative into a tight spot lies in their inability to retrieve objects. Old and well-defined spirits like Shifty can move things, but only with a basic level of control. Think your stock Hollywood levitation routine.

To overcome that limitation, I've developed an augmentation potion that hones Shifty's fine motor skills. Unfortunately, I used Drain-O for the base.

Now, bear with me. It's a matter of drawing on the principle of reversal. I chose a substance designed to push things through a limited space and re-engineered it to bring them back out instead. Even though I've continued to tinker with the recipe, I haven't been able to get rid of the unfortunate greening effect.

Time to call Shifty's bluff. I stood and said, "Well, if you're not interested, there are other spirits for hire."

The moonshiner's tone changed fast. "Now just hold on there, Mattie girl. I didn't say I *wouldn't* do it. I reckon you got yourself a good reason to want to know what's down in that there pipe."

"I do. It could help solve a murder."

That won me a grimy, wagging index finger. "Now there you go. Just like a woman. We wouldn't a'been standing here jawing if'n you'd told me that part *first*. Being as how I'm a good God fearing man with a respect for the law, of course I'll help you catch the black-hearted killer."

Rolling my eyes over the law-abiding part, I deadpanned, "My mistake. Meet me at the Nostalgia Nook at 2 a.m. Watch for my car and follow me to the spot without showing yourself until we're under cover. No scaring the tourists for the fun of it."

Rubbing his hands in anticipation, he said, "And you'll bring my pay?"

"One Mason jar of shine and 5 minutes to drink it," I said, "but not at the Lodge. I'll bring the shine up here when the case is over, but I swear to Hecate if you shoot me again you don't get a single drop."

I had a good reason for wanting to pay Shifty in private. Press and I had only now gotten on good terms—personally and professionally. He didn't need to catch me dispensing illegal hooch, especially when I had no intention of telling him where I acquire the shine.

Having sealed the deal with Shifty, I strolled back down the trail, enjoying the chance to stretch my legs. I had time to get home, take a nap since we were in for a long night, and make a batch of potato salad.

When a fairy extends an invitation for you to come on his land and dance to his music, you don't show up empty-handed.

Besides, what you regard as a side dish has far more significance in my world. Consider this your cultural lesson for the day: in the South, we take our potato salad *very* seriously. Keep reading.

Chapter 17

LET'S TALK ABOUT THE potato salad. There's more to our lives in Miller's Cove than creating a retro tourist destination. Yes, the past has become present for us, but sometimes we like to let our paranormal hair down.

If you're thinking of Rapunzel, stop. That's a fairy tale. I'm talking about living, breathing Southern paranormals who have built a community with social standards. Potato salad is a standard.

There are serious decisions to be made in the preparation of potato salad, the principle choice being mustard or mayonnaise. The Tucker women use mustard. The inclusion of hard-boiled eggs is non-negotiable, and pickles or pickle relish is unacceptable.

I may be a snob, but I'm inherently suspicious of a cook who would put pickle relish in potato salad when everyone knows it belongs in the deviled eggs.

Taking a bowl of potato salad to the Jones picking was an active defense of family honor. I needed folks to taste that potato salad and pronounce the quality to be as good as my Mama's and her Mama's before her. Not being a full-fledged kitchen witch does not get me off the potato salad hook.

Pressure to perform aside, I love working in the room that will always be "Mama's kitchen" to me. Using the big mixing bowls and cast iron cookware handed down through generations of Tucker women makes me feel closer to those maternal ancestors.

Legend has it that a witch never walks alone because she's surrounded by all the women who came before her, the weavers of the tapestry of her family's magic.

The ancestors are my only true coven.

Sometimes when I'm rolling out a pie crust or kneading bread, I feel Mama looking over my shoulder and seize the opportunity to talk with her.

A ghost who has business with you doesn't like to be ignored, but the ancestors won't tolerate the brush off from some upstart descendant who happens to still be drawing breath.

They're not on this plane with us, but they visit frequently, usually at times when we need them and don't realize it. Mama tends to show up when I've missed an important clue on a case and could use a nudge in the right direction.

More times than not, however, I don't get what she's trying to tell me until some other factor has solved the riddle. That doesn't mean Mama isn't a good communicator, but rather that I'm a poor listener and interpreter.

That afternoon when a jar of grape jelly fell off a pantry shelf and shattered, I took the accident as a sign of nothing more than my own clumsiness. The purple mess didn't splatter my pants, saving me from re-conceptualizing a complete outfit, so I cleaned everything up and went back to peeling potatoes.

When my salad sat cooling in the ice box, I stretched out on the sofa in the den and dozed off for a long nap.

The exercise of reviewing the case with Raylene at the Deja Vu had cleared my mind enough that I could sleep without restless churning—a method that works great for butter and does nothing for shut eye.

I woke up excited about the coming evening. In theory we were going to the Joneses so I could speak with Remi away from any prying ears at the Lodge, but I love a good fairy party.

People who don't know how to get to the Jones land will never find the gate. The will-o'-the-wisps see to that. In these parts you may hear the flickering elemental spirits who shelter on the Jones' land called ghost lights. They love to lead travelers astray, and guard the fairies' land in exchange for a safe haven.

The Miller's Cove fairies are human in appearance and size, with glittering, retractable wings. When they go home and cross the barrier protecting their clan holdings, however, they revert to their natural miniature stature. The tallest among them stands around 8 inches.

In the Old Country, fairies lived in rowan groves. Here in Tennessee they cling close to the tree's near relative, the Mountain Ash. The Miller's Cove clans, the Joneses and the Monroes, are trooping fairies who are happiest in large groups.

They're all related, which makes them even more prone to feuding. You just think Thanksgiving with Crazy Uncle Ted is a nightmare. Fairies are easily offended by humans and other paranormals, but they whip one another into actual blood rages, which is why the two groups keep to opposite ends of the county.

The Joneses are skilled musicians, who host open-door parties at least twice a month. The Monroes are masters at mountain crafts and healing.

Granny witches are common in Appalachia, but Aunt Saro Monroe puts them all to shame. She keeps a properly outfitted medical office in town and sometimes consults with Santos.

The real healings, however, take place under the old ash tree that shelters her tiny cabin high up in the branches. Aunt Saro is the only Monroe welcome among the Joneses.

The pleasant anticipation I felt when I awakened was multi-layered. As I brushed out my hair and let it fall around my shoulders, I was thinking about looking pretty for Press, being among my fairy friends, and meeting up with Shifty.

My gut told me that the moonshiner would help us find something that might result in a major step toward a solution to Frank's murder.

At a quarter of 8, I rolled up in Raylene's driveway, but my early arrival didn't faze her. "Get in this house and help me choose. I've got it down to three looks," she declared, holding the screen door open for me.

I rejected the first ensemble out of hand—white polka dots on black does not stealth mode make.

Raylene sadly agreed. "I was afraid of that, but polka dot prints are so festive I thought I'd risk it. How about this one?"

She snapped her fingers and produced navy trousers and a blouse a shade or two lighter. The deep pleats accentuated her trim figure as did the top's v-neck and exaggerated collar.

"That's the one," I said. "Maybe add a necklace?"

More finger snapping produced a gold oval locket about the size of a 50 cent piece and matching earrings.

Surveying herself in the mirror, Raylene said, "I feel naked without a pin, but this light fabric will pucker, so I guess I'm ready. Do we need anything else? Maybe a flashlight?"

"No, there should be enough light around the drain. A flashlight would only call attention to us. Let's go. I have a big bowl of potato salad in the backseat."

"Oh, gosh. I'm glad you said that. I almost forgot my sandwich platter." She bustled off toward the kitchen still talking. "I fixed ham and chicken salad—and pimento cheese."

My face lit up. "Did you make extra of the pimento cheese?"

A scoffing noise floated out of the kitchen along with the sound of tin foil being ripped off the roll. "Silly, of course I did. I sent the bowl straight to your refrigerator."

My potato salad is good, but Raylene's pimento cheese constitutes a golden, gooey legend.

On the way out to the Joneses, she said, "I feel sort of bad having fun like this in the middle of a murder case."

I jerked the wheel and ran us onto the side of the road when a voice from the back seat said, "At least one of you has a conscience."

Raylene twisted to look over her shoulder. "Well, would you look at that. So you finally decided to let me see you, huh?"

"Darn right I did, lady," Frank shot back. "That was a mean trick you pulled on Vanessa with that Aquatic Nettle doohickey."

I was too busy keeping the tires on the asphalt and deep breathing to calm my thudding heart to referee the exchange.

"Her name," Raylene said, "is Aqua Netta and don't blame me. Talk to your private investigator over there."

Out of the corner of my eye I saw an index finger with a red-lacquered nail point in my direction.

"Hey!" I protested. "Way to throw me under the bus."

Then, glaring at Frank in the rear view mirror, I said, "Do *not* pop in like that again when I'm driving. What are you doing here anyway?"

The ghost wavered. "Vanessa and Floyd are at that night club with the piano player. The one with the fat guy in a fez sitting at one of the front tables. I think he might have a monkey, too. Anyway, I wasn't going to just float around all night and watch them have a good time and I don't have anyone else to talk to. Can I stay with you two?"

I cut a look in Raylene's direction, but she shook her head. Message received. Dealing with Frank was on me.

"You can stay," I said, "but you'll see some things you might not understand."

"At least I won't be alone even if the two of you would rather go to a party than solve my murder."

That's the kind of self-pity that doesn't work on me and goes straight to my tough-talking pal's soft heart. "Oh, Mr. Reynolds," Raylene said. "You're not alone."

That tiny crumb of sympathy was all the ghost needed to forget his upset over the Aqua Netta incident. "My name is Frank."

"Frank," she said, "We're not going to this party because we don't care what happened to you."

"Then why are you going?" he demanded.

My turn. "The maître d' from the Nostalgia Nook will be at the party after the restaurant closes. He thinks someone at the Lodge might be stealing credit card information from guests. Do you know anything about that?"

The ghost shook his head. "We had dinner in our room, not the restaurant. I had them put the charge on the tab."

Okay, that cogent answer was a good sign. We had the spirit in a clear state of mind, which I didn't intend to waste. "What happened when the food was delivered to your room?"

"The room service guy brought the cart inside and set the table for us. We ate, and then put the dishes back on the cart and rolled it outside the door for him to pick up later."

That all sounded perfectly normal until Frank abruptly lost focus and said in a detached tone, "Vanessa hates bugs."

Careful to keep my voice level and calm, I said, "A bug got in your room?"

Fading to a pale shadow of himself, Frank said, "I didn't see it. When do we get to the party?"

"It won't be long," I assured him. "Just sit back and enjoy the ride. Conserve your energy."

The ghost did as I suggested, but his ability to manifest had dipped so low his form disappeared halfway into the backseat cushions.

"I thought we covered the bug angle," Raylene said under her breath.

"Normal bugs, yes," I whispered back, "but not paranormal bugs."

We try to keep the supernatural population of Miller's Cove in the sentient creature lane. Other than an unfortunate incident with a pack of Egyptian scarabs that animated themselves out of the King Tut exhibit in Nashville a few years back, I didn't know of any unnatural vermin infestations in the state.

I'm not the kind of woman who looks for a man to kill the bugs, but I made up my mind right then and there. If some preternatural creepy crawly picked up an ax and flew it into Frank Reynolds skull, I would be more than happy for Press to handle catching and killing the dang thing.

Chapter 18

BECAUSE I'M A TUCKER, the will-o'-the-wisps not only let us on the Jones land, one of the elementals served as an escort. The bright light bobbed a few feet ahead of the Dodge's high beams as we bounced down the long dark lane.

The road wound up to a hollow where a stone barn sits nestled in an ash grove. Architecturally unique for the region, the fairies built the solid "big house" to meet the needs of their full-sized guests.

The Jones troop may reserve their acreage as a sanctuary that allows them to live in their authentic form, but they love to share with friends of all sizes. They make a genuine effort to ensure everyone's comfort.

When I was little, Daddy brought me to the Jones place to fish in the big creek that tumbles down through a rocky cleft in the mountainside. Before we could wet a hook, fairies would start joining us in groups of twos and threes.

While we fished, they played with the dragonflies and raced chattering squirrels into the tree tops. No matter where I went, I always had a book with me. Ultimately Daddy would doze off over his pole, and I'd prop mine between some rocks so I could sit back against a tree trunk and read.

On many an occasion, Punk Jones sat there with me, legs dangling over my shoulder waiting for me to turn the page. Even a kid like me who grew up surrounded by witches regards fairy culture as magical. I'm proud to call the Joneses my friends and to be welcome among them.

All around the stone barn lights twinkled high in the trees, shining through the windows of the fairies' arboreal dwellings. Whimsical cottages sit tucked up there in the limbs anchored against knot holes or built along the thickest branches.

Tending lush moss lawns and tiny transplanted flowers, most fairies are content to never come down to earth. Only a few, like Punk, transform and make the drive into town to work for the benefit of the whole clan.

For the most part, though, the fairies maintain a self-sufficient, peaceful society sharing honey with the bees and fruit from the wild orchards.

At that very moment, I knew that fairy elders rocked on their front porches and looked down on the partygoers through the big sky lights cut in the barn roof. Like Miller's Cove residents, the fairies live in a past of their own choosing—a storybook village in the trees.

We found three dozen or so cars parked on the newly mown grass. When I stepped out of the Dodge, that fresh cut smell filled my nostrils. With it came the aroma of fragrant blooms and pungent herbs. Any spot a fairy troop calls home teems with vibrant life.

The barn doors, thrown open to the evening air, offered a tableau of the festivities in progress. Lilting music mingled with buzzing voices and laughter.

All mountain music derives from Celtic songs, which the fairies themselves composed in the Old Land. They still write music, but even the newest tune rings with ancient resonance on their cherished instruments.

Full-sized dancers circled the ground floor while fairies filled the rafters above them, wings flashing among strings of lights. Raylene and I made our way around the room to the food tables.

We added our contributions to the already impressive bounty. Friends waved and called out to us. Punk Jones flourish his fiddle bow in our direction from the elevated bandstand.

Frank held a levitating presence beside us, head back, staring up at the fairies with a slack jaw. Leaning closer to the ghost, I said, "How are you doing with all this?"

"They're so beautiful," he gasped, never lowering his eyes. "I never thought anything like this could be real. I wish Vanessa could see this."

When I felt a hand at the small of my back, I turned to find Press beside us.

"Mattie, Raylene, you both look lovely."

He'd changed out of his ubiquitous double-breasted suit in favor of gray trousers and a plaid sport shirt. The casual attire softened the vampire's countenance and afforded me a glimpse of the country boy he'd been before he left Miller's Cove for Chicago.

"Hey, Press," Raylene said. "Frank's here, too. I can see him now."

"Evening, Frank," Press said in the ghost's general direction.

I relayed Frank's response, adding my own greeting. "Hi, Press. I don't think I've ever seen you wear anything but a suit."

The vampire grinned. "At least you didn't say *stuffed* suit."

Before the party, I might well have described Press as stiff and uptight. Most of the time since the day we met the two of us have been at odds with one another.

Now, I found myself in the company of a relaxed man who gallantly insisted on eating my potato salad and no other when we filled our plates.

I've never been shy about showing my lack of knowledge regarding any subject. Learning cures ignorance. Questions trigger learning. When I don't know something, I ask.

Watching Press take his first bite, I said, "I'm confused. I thought you were on a liquid diet."

"I was for years until I taught myself to eat solid food again. It won't keep me alive, but having a regular meal makes me feel more normal, especially in social settings. And I think it puts other people at ease, too."

We'd taken our plates outside and claimed seats at one of several merrily crackling fire pits at the back of the barn. We were mostly alone and Press was in a talkative mood. I ran with the moment in case he clammed up again.

"How did you teach yourself to eat?" I asked curiously.

"Slowly," he laughed. "In the beginning more came up than stayed down. I had to find something that would jumpstart my taste buds and make me want more."

"What did the trick?"

"Sardines covered in cream cheese and hot sauce."

Wrinkling my nose, I said, "That's disgusting."

Press took a bite out of one of Raylene's pimento cheese sandwiches and considered my evaluation. "Yeah, I guess by anyone's standards the combination would be nauseating, but that was the first food I'd really tasted since the steak I ate the night I was turned. I wolfed down a whole tin and went looking for more."

"And you didn't get sick?"

"No, but every alley cat in town fell in love with me on first sniff."

He was being so forthcoming, I said, without thinking, "Please tell me you like cats."

"I love cats—dogs, goats, horses, birds, goldfish. I'm a total pushover for animals of any kind."

My next question wasn't planned, but it begged to be asked. "Then you don't..."

"Take blood from animals? No. Santos handles my pantry."

That took a minute for me to sort out. "*Oh!* The monthly blood drives."

"The good witch doctor puts a few pints aside for me. I can't very well sink my fangs into the people I'm sworn to protect and serve."

"Sure you can. Politicians do it all the time."

Press put on a serious face, but his eyes sparkled. "I may be a vampire, Mattie, but do *not* compare me to a politician."

We both dissolved into peals of laughter. Unsolved ax murder aside, I was having a wonderful time and, judging from what I could see, so was Raylene.

She'd been on the dance floor almost from the moment we arrived. For his part, Frank had discovered the number one pastime of ghosts the world over—eavesdropping. By the end of the evening, he'd be an expert on all the local gossip.

Press and I danced several times, but we always found our way back to conversation by the fire pit. That's where we were when I spotted Raylene threading through the crowd with Remi close behind.

Unlike Press, the Barbgazi couldn't bring himself to go casual. He looked ready to show us to a table and suggest a good wine.

"I snagged Remi when he got here," Raylene said, claiming a seat. "I told him you wanted to speak with him."

Remi removed a white handkerchief from his pocket and dusted off the remaining seat. "Not that speaking with you isn't a pleasure, Mattie," he said, arranging himself, "but I am curious about the topic of the evening."

"It's okay, Remi," Press said. "I asked Mattie to speak with you. You all excuse me now. I'm going to go find a cold beer."

Watching the vampire stride away, Remi said, "Why do I feel I am not in possession of all the relevant facts?"

"Because you're not," I said. "Mayor Leonard asked Press not to pursue your concerns about potential identity theft at the Lodge."

Comprehension registered in the Barbgazi's eyes. "Ah! So Preston will comply with the request because he is a good soldier and you will do the proverbial dirty work of the unpopular investigation."

"Exactly. Anything you might want to say to me, you can say in front of Raylene."

"But, of course," Remi said, nodding at her. "I must begin by observing that this meddling on the part of the mayor does not surprise me."

"Why is that?"

"Because no one has worked harder to redirect the course of Miller's Cove into a prosperous, purposeful community. He would not want scandal to mar the town's image as an honest haven for tourists. I will tell you what I know."

Over the next few minutes we listened as Remi told us the same story he'd shared with Press. Guests received bills at checkout that accurately reflected their purchases, but within a week of their departure, additional charges were processed on their cards.

Some reported the discrepancies, and then had a change of heart saying they'd forgotten the purchases in question. Others never said a word, and simply paid for goods and services they never received. Remi had no way of knowing if more fraudulent charges were made on the cards later on.

"And no one at the Lodge takes the guests' card information at any point during their stay?" I asked.

Remi sat up straighter. "Most certainly not. Handling charge cards would not be correct to the period we work to accurately reproduce for the benefit of our clients."

"Come on, Remi," Raylene said. "You know everyone on staff at the lodge. Surely you have a suspect."

A cagey look came into the Barbgazi's eyes. "Let us suppose for the moment that someone of my acquaintance might be able to shed light on the crime at hand. Let us also suppose that the individual in question could be subject to collateral blame for innocent participation. Could an arrangement be brokered to ensure that my contact would not suffer consequences from either legal system?"

In Miller's Cove we abide by two sets of laws: human and paranormal. By the careful framing of his question, Remi was telling us that we were also looking at a violation of supernatural statutes—which meant we were talking about more than credit card fraud.

"You're asking for an immunity deal for your friend," I said.

"I am."

"Can you give me any further details?"

"Not until I have some sense of a guarantee in place. The friend in question is in a vulnerable position."

"Okay. That's not something Press is going to want to discuss in a crowd like this. Give me a few hours. I'll get back to you tomorrow."

"Excellent," he said, standing and buttoning his coat. "Now, am I to understand, Raylene, that you prepared pimento cheese for the evening?"

"I did," she said, standing and taking the arm he offered, "and I hid some just for you. Mattie, are you coming?"

As we walked back into the barn, Press shot me an inquisitive look over the shoulders of the men with whom he was drinking beer. I shrugged and mouthed the words "tomorrow morning."

The vampire frowned, but nodded and went back to his conversation. Raylene and I would have to leave soon to make our appointment with Shifty. Maybe whatever my gut told me was down that drain would shed some light on who or what Remi was protecting.

Chapter 19

I POINTED THE DODGE down the lane toward the country road that would take us to the Nostalgia Nook the back way. Raylene and I were alone in the car. Frank didn't answer when I waved to him signaling our departure, so we left him at the barn. He seemed to be enjoying listening in on conversations more than anything else that had happened to him since his unfortunate demise.

Raylene waited until the lights of the party barn had disappeared behind us to say, "Well, that talk with Remi didn't go the way I expected it would. Here you thought he was in danger and it turns out he's protecting someone else."

"I'm guessing a person caught up in the middle of the credit card scheme with no way out came to him for help. The Barbgazi are known for their huge hearts."

We bounced out onto the paved road and drove a mile or so before Raylene said, "Credit card fraud doesn't violate paranormal law."

I knew we'd have to address that complication sooner or later. "I know."

Raylene reached up and started toying with the chain of her necklace. "If I were Press, I'd want to know why you decided to wait until tomorrow to share that detail with me."

Best friends are supposed to be part of a person's moral compass, but I wouldn't have minded if she'd left me to navigate by the seat of my britches on this particular conundrum.

When I didn't answer, I could feel Raylene's eyes studying me in the dashboard lights. Those mental gears of hers were cranking along faster than the Dodge, and I had the speedometer resting on 60 mph.

"Mattie Tucker," she said at last. "Are you holding back on him because we have an appointment with Shifty and you didn't want to risk Press finding out?"

Squirming, I said, "Of course not." I tried to sound amused and dismissive, but the words came out guilty as sin.

"Don't you even think about lying to me," Raylene warned. "It won't work."

I tried again. "We may find something at the Lodge that will help us figure out who Remi is trying to help."

"Uh *huh*," Raylene said, emphasizing the second syllable in a way I didn't like.

"What?"

Still twining and untwining the necklace on the fingers of her right hand, she said, "You're a skinny gal, Mattie, but if Shifty does find something, I don't think you're going to be able to convince Press that you went down that drain yourself."

She'd hit straight on the weakest spot in my already rickety non-plan. "Do you think he'd believe we used a sewer camera?"

"Not period correct."

"Trained rat?"

She stopped playing with the necklace and turned in the seat to look at me. "You are not serious. You think Press is going to believe you employed a rodent to do your dirty work after you shot the poor man last year over a rat during the homecoming game?"

That touched off a long string of mental profanity on my part. I'd conveniently forgotten about that instance of trying to get the vampire killed.

"It was only a flesh wound," I said, "and yes, the rat was disgusting, but it also had our evidence in its mouth."

"Mattie, be practical."

"Raylene," I said seriously, "trust me on this one. Keeping Shifty and Press apart is me being practical."

She sighed. "Okay, but I'm just saying that if you're planning to go on working with Shifty *and* Press, they're going to run into one another sooner than later. Wouldn't you like to get ahead of that?"

I kept my eyes on the road and my mouth shut. Raylene knew she had a strong argument, but I wasn't backing down.

"Come on Mattie," she said. "How bad could getting those two together really be?"

Several dozen disaster scenarios skipped through my brain. "Ask me that when Shifty peppers your hide with ghost shot. I'd rather have a bad case of chiggers any day than get in the middle of that feud."

"Careful," Raylene warned. "The Universe might think you meant that."

Good point. Chiggers itch worse than ghost shot. I jumped to cover my metaphysical bases. "I don't want chiggers," I said with conviction, "but I also don't want to be the one to help Shifty and Press work out their issues."

"There has to be more to that story," Raylene said, "or they wouldn't both be holding on to the grudge this long."

From the backseat, Frank said, "There's always more to the story."

Jerking the wheel, I yelled, "*Frank!* I told you not to do that!"

"Sorry," the ghost apologized. "Is the town mayor really a werewolf?"

Frank's pop-in non sequiturs were starting to grate on my nerves, but this time he got me out of the hot seat with Raylene. For that favor, I hopped right on the rabbit trail with him, but first I glanced in the rear view to check the spirit's condition. He had good color and a well-defined outline. Gossip-mongering appeared to agree with him.

"Why?" I asked. "Did you hear someone talking about Mayor Leonard?"

"Why do people call him Buckshot?" Frank asked.

Ignoring the snicker from the passenger seat, I said, "He doesn't like to discuss his nickname."

Frank accepted the evasion at face value. "Okay. Well, I heard a lady saying he does good work with whipple."

I didn't see that monkey wrench coming. The only whipple that crawled out of my memory was George Whipple. The fictional grocery store manager hawked Charmin toilet paper in ads from 1964 to 1985.

"What's a whipple?" I asked.

Our backseat apparition was doing an unusually good job of staying on topic. "It's an acronym. Werewolf Protection League. W-P-L. Whipple."

Cutting my eyes over at Raylene, I said, "Do you have any idea what he's talking about?"

"I've heard of the group. They help relocate werewolves with assimilation problems."

Of all the paranormal species trying to make their way in the modern world, I feel the worst for shifters. There are two types: voluntary and involuntary.

The classifications tell the story. Voluntary shifters change at will. Werewolves are involuntary—at the mercy of the lunar phases. That makes keeping up appearances challenging, personally and professionally.

"You mean the group fosters them?" I asked. "Like stray dogs?"

"I'm not sure how the program works," Raylene said, "but that's more or less the idea."

Don't think for one minute that I don't support that kind of work, because I do, but bringing an unvetted newcomer into Miller's Cove violates what we call, The Bubble.

Before anyone can move to town, they have to go through an application and approval process. Not everyone can handle living eighty or so years in the past while protecting the truth about our paranormal population from the outside world.

Raylene's mind had gone to the same place. "It would explain a lot," she said.

"A lot about what?" I countered. "Frank's murder, the credit card scam, or who Remi is protecting?"

"All of it."

"Werewolves don't typically kill people with axes," I said.

"No," she agreed, "but they are woodsy. It's not impossible."

"How would Buckshot bring someone into town and hide them?"

"He wouldn't have to hide them. He's the mayor. He signs the approval forms."

Frank, following the tone if not the content of the exchange, said, "Did I do something that helped?"

When I started to answer, I caught sight of the ghost in the mirror. Whatever battery that charged him up at the barn had run down to empty. He looked as thin and fragile as a soggy Kleenex in allergy season.

"You did, Frank," I assured him. "Thank you. It's okay if you want to blip out for awhile."

"Maybe I will," he said, his voice wavering like a bad radio signal. "Nice people rescue dogs."

With that, he disappeared entirely. Up ahead, I saw the sign for the Nostalgia Nook."

"Frank's not wrong," Raylene said. "If Buckshot did perform some sort of werewolf rescue, he must have had a good reason for keeping the paperwork under the table. And if that wolf got in over his or her head with the credit card thing, Remi's trying another kind of rescue working out an immunity deal."

"If that's true, Buckshot and Remi are both too kind hearted for their own good," I said. "But one thing's for sure, neither one of them is involved with murder or fraud. I'd bet money on that."

Among her many good qualities, Raylene is also a betting woman. "I'd take some of that action in a heartbeat," she said. "Buckshot and Remi are not the bad guys, but that doesn't help us much. We're sitting on a pile of puzzle pieces with no glue to hold them together. Now what?"

Flipping on the blinker to turn into the Lodge parking lot, I said, "We send a dead moonshiner down a pipe and hope he comes up with something sticky."

Chapter 20

SINCE THE HIGHWAY WAS deserted and the three-quarter moon provided enough glow for me to drive, I cut the Dodge's headlamps before turning into the Nostalgia Nook parking lot.

I rolled into the same spot as the day of Frank's murder. We let ourselves out of the car as quietly as possible, meeting up at the back bumper.

Scanning rows of darkened windows, Raylene whispered, "Looks like all the guests have turned in for the night."

"That's the idea. Come on. We're supposed to meet Shifty at the ice machine—or at least where it used to be before Santos and his boys hauled it into the lab. Follow me."

We crossed the parking lot and approached the crime scene. No signs remained to suggest anything unusual had happened on the spot—certainly not that a man had lost his life there.

Even in the half light I could make out the silver circle of the drain cover set into the concrete walkway. Seconds later, Shifty materialized. I was ready for his arrival, putting a finger to my lips and shaking my head.

The ghost got the message, answering with a gap-toothed grin, but otherwise staying quiet. He did waggle his fingers in Raylene's direction by way of a greeting, which she answered with a wave.

Niceties out of the way, Shifty propped his shotgun against the wall, leaned casually beside it, and crossed his arms. This was not our first covert caper. He knew what came next and how long it would take.

Motioning for Raylene to move closer, I took a slender bottle of salt from the pocket of my trousers. Starting at the wall, I sprinkled a line to the edge of the sidewalk, made a ninety degree turn, went about five feet, and then headed back to the wall again. From there, I traced along the bricks until I was back where I started.

Magically speaking, I'd drawn a "circle" that in this case was a rectangle. A proper circle would have protected us and repelled an attacker. But for the task at hand, all I needed was a simulacrum mask to prevent our activities from being observed.

I put away the bottle and held the fingertips of both hands inches apart. Releasing my control, I let my electromagnetic field flare. When blue arcs crackled between my fingertips, I knelt by the salt line and whispered a few words in Latin.

The spell directed the current into the mineral. Green flame spread left and right, rising as the fire flowed along the barrier I'd transcribed. In the space of a heartbeat a pulsing jade curtain surrounded our work area.

To anyone on the outside, the brick wall and sidewalk would look normal and deserted. We were now free to speak without worrying about being overheard and we had enough light to work.

"Great Jehoshaphat, Mattie girl," Shifty cackled. "I do fair enjoy watching you cast a spell. Miss Raylene, right nice to see you again."

"Hey, Shifty," she answered. 'Mighty nice of you to help out tonight."

The jagged grin returned. "I get paid real well for my generous nature."

"Don't forget that," I said, producing a second bottle filled with green and white crystals. "This is the part of the job you don't like."

The moonshiner straightened. "Go on, Mattie, douse me good. There's worse things can happen to a feller than turning green."

Like being blown up by your own illegal still.

Uncorking the bottle, I sprinkled the contents liberally over Shifty. The crystals sizzled when they made contact with his ectoplasm and raised patches of foam that put out a soft celery glow.

As we watched, the light filled every wrinkle and crease of the ghost's clothing before flowing over his skin.

"Hey!" he said, sounding pleased and surprised. "You done been working on your recipe, ain't you? This time it don't feel like a bunch of ants crawling all over me and look. I ain't nearly as green as I was last time."

Hopefully that didn't mean I'd weakened the potion's strength to the point of rendering it useless. "Let's try this version out in action," I suggested. "Why don't you give a shot at removing the drain cover?"

"Sure thing," he said, unsheathing a hunting knife from his belt. When he moved to work the tip under the grate, instead of passing through the material, the blade caught. With an easy twist of his wrist, Shifty raised the cover and used his other hand to move it to the side, exposing the open pipe.

The ghost crowed with delight. "Yeehaw! Would you look at that? Slicker than lard hitting a hot skillet."

The degree of dexterity the action required made the hours I spent refining the mixture more than worth the effort. Shifty should have the necessary control to bring anything he found in the pipe up to the surface.

"Okay, we're in business. Are you ready to go diving, Shifty?"

"Sure am," he said. "You all watch my shotgun for me."

After we assured him that the non-corporeal firearm would be safe with us, the ghost raised his arms over his head and threw himself into a spin, picking up velocity with each rotation.

When he'd thinned out to the diameter of the drain, Shifty executed a perfect dive, disappearing down the pipe head first.

Watching the last wisp of the moonshiner vanish, Raylene said, with a wistful expression, "I wish I could get thin that fast."

"Please," I scoffed. "You never gain an ounce."

"Honey, it's the pounds I worry about, not the ounces. How does he turn around when he's down there?"

"Beats me," I admitted. "I think he sorta turns himself inside out."

Raylene shuddered at the image my words painted. "I'm sorry I asked."

A sucking gurgle sounded in the pipe. Shifty shot out of the confined space so fast, he splatted against the concrete overhang, flattened out like a pancake, and landed in a viscous puddle at our feet.

"Uh, Shifty?" I ventured tentatively. "You doing okay there, buddy?"

The ectoplasm gathered into a blob that turned into a pair of well-worn boots, then patched pants, a belt, a work shirt, and finally a complete moonshiner.

"*Tarnations!*" Shifty, exclaimed, sticking a finger in his right ear and scratching vigorously. "I am getting a dang sight too long of tooth to be a'doing this kind of thing."

I made a commiserating noise in the back of my throat before forging ahead with business. "Not to be insensitive, Shifty, but did you find anything?"

The ghost scowled at me. "Hold your horses there, missy. Let a man get his bones back where they belong."

It took everything I had not to mention that he had no bones, but I restrained myself and waited. As Raylene and I watched, Shifty fidgeted, knocked drain water out of his ears, and went through an intense coughing fit.

When he was done, he held out his hand and said, "Reckon this is what you was a'looking for, ain't it?"

A single round cut diamond of quite respectable size sat suspended on the spirit's palm. I gingerly picked up the stone, holding it between my thumb and forefinger. The pulsating light of the privacy spell caught the gem's facets and made them flash.

"*Wow!*" I breathed. "That has to be at least a carat."

"Try two," Raylene said. "Maybe even a D grade."

Scholastically I knew the letter meant bad news, but I had no idea how it related to the quality of pricey rocks. "Is that a good thing?"

"It's an expensive thing. Diamonds that are rated as a D grade are colorless and rare. That's why this one looks so much like ice."

Her knowledge impressed me. "Listen to you. How come you know so much about diamonds?"

She sniffed. "Because a no count man tried to pass off a cubic zirconium on me once—emphasis on *once*."

I could well imagine the rapid end-of-relationship fireworks that dumb move engendered. "What do you suppose it's worth?" I asked, turning the stone and watching light play through its facets.

"Well," she said critically, "I'm just guessing, but probably north of thirty thousand."

That almost knocked me over. *"Dollars?"* I squeaked.

Raylene gave me a wry look. "That's usually how people pay for jewelry, sugar. At least in this country."

Shifty let out a low whistle. "Shore is a purty thing, ain't it?"

Moving with exaggerated care, I took the empty salt bottle out of my pocket and handed it to Raylene. "Open that for me, will you?"

When she pulled out the cork stopper, I *very* carefully dropped the diamond inside and closed the bottle again.

Giving me a concerned look, Raylene said, "Mattie, are you okay? You're greener than Shifty."

"I'm fine. I just didn't want to drop the diamond. I think I know what got Frank killed."

She arched an eyebrow. "You think someone murdered him over a single diamond?"

I shook my head. "No. That single diamond is what Frank was trying to find in the ice machine. You said it yourself. A rock with that kind of clarity would disappear against the ice cubes, especially at night."

"So what did get him killed?"

"The rest of the diamonds he was carrying."

Still looking skeptical, Raylene said, "How do you know there were more stones?"

"There had to be. Floyd must have sold them in exchange for those uncirculated $500 bills he tried to use in the clock shop."

The sound of a car engine made us all turn toward the parking lot. A local yellow cab pulled under the Lodge's covered entrance. Floyd and Vanessa got out. Floyd paid the fare and then the two disappeared into the lobby.

"Now where do you suppose those two are going?" Raylene asked. "It's almost three o'clock in the morning."

"I don't know, but before we confront them, I want to talk to Press. Let's get home and get some sleep. I'll track him down first thing come daylight. Thank you, Shifty. You outdid yourself this time."

The moonshiner beamed at me. "My pleasure, Mattie girl. You don't go forgetting my shine now, you hear?"

"Don't worry," I assured him. "I'll deliver your hooch as soon as we get this case wrapped up."

"Fair enough," he said, retrieving his shotgun. "Evening, Mattie, Miss Raylene." With that he started across the parking lot, growing fainter with each step until he disappeared entirely.

After I broke the circle and dispersed the salt, Raylene and I climbed into the Dodge and drove back to town. The late hour and the excitement of the night was catching up with us both. Raylene barely managed to stay awake until we reached her house, giving me a sleepy hug before she stumbled up the front walk and went inside.

I managed to get myself home safely, but I was so exhausted I didn't even bother going upstairs. I fell asleep on the couch in the den with the diamond still in my pocket. Which is where I was when Press woke me up at dawn knocking on the front door.

Chapter 21

PRESS HADN'T CHANGED clothes either. Somehow his casual look struck me as even more incongruous in the pale dawn light. The sun had barely started to rise over the mountains to the east, but the vampire already wore dark shades to protect his eyes.

In some ways nature gave Press a face tailor-made to deliver bad news. From the resigned set of that square jaw and the grim line of his mouth, Press's visage said, *"Brace yourself!"*

Now fully awake under the weight of growing apprehension, I dispensed with any niceties. "What?"

"Remi D'Aboville is dead."

The words suspended themselves between us. They seemed to both hold on to the night that had slipped behind us and reach for the new day on the horizon—a day Remi would never see.

Looking back on that shocking revelation, I'm still bothered that I didn't immediately say something to memorialize the Barbgazi. I didn't think to mention the pride he took in his work at the restaurant or to recall the unabashed joy that infused his face when he looked at the mountains.

Instead, I went for a prosaic response maybe because I couldn't bear to do anything more in the moment. "I'll make coffee."

It's a straight shot from the front door to the kitchen. I almost covered the whole distance before I realized Press wasn't behind me.

I looked back and saw him framed in the doorway, hands hanging loosely at his side. "Are you coming in?"

"Are you *asking* me in?"

When you're interested in a vampire, you study the etiquette. Had *The Well-Mannered Fang* let me down? "Isn't that a myth? That vampires need an invitation to enter a house?"

He shifted awkwardly, then removed his glasses. His eyes were red-rimmed and raw. "Yes, it's a myth, but...well...I've never been to your home before."

How had this complicated man gone from grouchy nemesis to socially uncertain house guest in two days? If he needed an invitation to feel comfortable with me, I was happy to issue one.

"Press, would you like to come in and have a cup of coffee with me so we can talk about Remi?"

Relief registered on his face. "Thank you. I'd like that very much." I think he almost stopped himself from saying what came next, but then decided to go on. The words melted my heart. "It's been a long couple of hours."

As he walked toward me, I heard the unspoken end of the sentence. *"Investigating the death of my friend."*

The vampire followed me into the kitchen, taking a seat at the table while I measured out the coffee and put the pot on the stove.

I opened the fridge and blankly stared at the contents. Should we eat? Would that delay the painful details a few minutes longer?

Behind me Press said, "Have you had any sleep?"

The clock set in the stove's back panel read 6:30. "A couple of hours on the den sofa."

I didn't have to look at Press. I *heard* the frown. "You left the Jones's place about 1:30. Did something happen on the way home?"

Some half comatose feminist principle at the back of my mind raised its head and said, *"It's none of his business when you got home."* I told the voice to shut up and go back to bed.

"Raylene and I met Shifty at the Nostalgia Nook. I asked him to look down the drain under the ice machine. How do you like your eggs?"

If Press disapproved of my methods, he decided to wait to say so. "Over easy. What did Shifty find?"

Balancing a carton of eggs atop a package of bacon, I closed the icebox door, took the bottle holding the diamond out of my pocket, and put it on the table.

The vampire picked up the container and examined the glittering gemstone.

"He found *that*," I said. "Was Remi killed at the Lodge?"

"Yes."

Even though I was afraid of the answer, I asked. "While we were outside at the drain?"

A man more given to coddling would have instantly assured me there was nothing we could have done. Press said, "What time did you all finish?"

"Around three in the morning."

"Santos estimates time of death was around four. We got the call at 4:30. I was playing poker with Punk and some other guys at the barn after the party broke up."

In my hand the eggs started to wobble in the carton. Bracing them before scrambled became our only menu option, I said, "How was Remi killed?"

Press respected me enough to shoot straight. "With a fire ax. The perp took it off the wall outside his office. Single blow to the head."

That detail penetrated my analytical processes. "Copycat or same killer?"

"We don't know yet."

When I didn't move, Press got up and reached for the bacon and eggs. "I can do that if you..."

When his fingers brushed mine, I swallowed against the painful lump that rose in my throat. "Thanks. Just, uh, just give me a few, okay?"

"Of course. Take your time."

I don't really remember stumbling upstairs, but the hot water in the shower slowly cleared the fog in my brain at the same time it washed the tears off my face. Slowly facts and time stamps started to arrange themselves as coherence replaced my sense of shock.

When I came back downstairs in fresh clothes, with the ends of my hair still damp, the scent of breakfast cooking hit me full on. My stomach growled; I needed more than wanted that cup of coffee.

Press must have used his sharp, vampiric hearing to time the food preparation. When I walked into the kitchen, he immediately put a piping hot plate of bacon and eggs on the table along with biscuits and gravy.

The counters and stove looked spotless. "You made all this *and* cleaned?"

"It gave me something else to think about," he admitted, filling our cups before joining me.

After several bites, I said, "For a guy who doesn't live on solid food, you're a good cook."

"I learned here and there along the way. Like I said, doing normal things helps a guy in my position keep up appearances."

I smiled at him. "This time it helped me, too. I don't have a weak stomach. Go on. Tell me what happened."

Press had been sitting on an inside straight when the phone in the barn rang. Punk, in his full-sized form for the card game, took the call. It was Jerry looking for Press with the news about Remi.

"We're not sure of the exact time Remi left the barn," Press said, "but it couldn't have been long after you and Raylene took off. Did you see his car on the road?"

"I drove the back way. If he took the regular route, he probably beat us there."

Whenever Remi arrived at the Lodge, he put his car in the underground garage and went to his office. "There were no signs of a struggle in the room," Press said. "The perp came up behind him."

That didn't sound right. "Where is Remi's desk in relation to the door?"

"It would be easier to show you. Jerry took the official crime scene photos, but I shot a second set in color for you with my phone. Are you ready to look at them?"

That was a little like asking the *Titanic* passengers if they were ready to go for a moonlight swim. No, I wasn't ready to see my friend dead, but it had to be done.

I stood and carried our dishes to the sink. "Let's go into my study. That's where I usually work on my cases."

More coffee seemed in order, so I topped off our cups before leading Press through the connecting door into the adjacent room.

When I flipped on the lights, appreciation registered on his face. He took in the dark paneling and overflowing bookcases with obvious approval. "This is nice."

"It's my favorite room in the house," I admitted. "Daddy used it for his work. After he died, I didn't change a thing. I always feel like he's keeping an eye on me when I'm in here."

Moving to the easy chair to the right of the hearth, I waved Press into its mate on the other side of the Persian rug. Before I sat, I switched on the electric logs.

Press nodded toward the grate. "I like those."

"Thanks. I can't stand looking at a black, empty fireplace regardless of the season."

Still soaking in the details of his surroundings, Press asked, "Was your father always a clockmaker?"

"No, by training, he was an archaeologist."

The vampire's face registered surprise. "How does an archaeologist wind up running a clock shop?"

"He was also a time witch. Clocks were a hobby before the town adopted the anachronism theme. I thought you knew my father."

The vampire grinned. "I did, but your family never had any run-ins with the law until you came along, so we were only passing acquaintances."

"Very funny."

"Your father's temporal powers gave him special insight into the past?"

"Exactly. Daddy studied at Vanderbilt. He traveled to digs when he was a younger man, but when I was born he wanted to be home more."

While we had been talking, I'd placed my coffee on the end table along with my iPhone. Now I used my magic to access the case diagram contained in the device, moving the information along a glowing ribbon of light. The data flattened out in the space between our chairs and the hearth.

Looking over at Press, I said, "May I have your phone?"

He handed me the iPhone without hesitation. "I'll have to install an app," I warned him.

"Go ahead. This won't be the last time we need to share case information. Just don't mess up my Words with Friends."

Both statements made me smile. "You shouldn't have told me that. You're going down, buddy. I am the queen of WWF. What's your username?"

"BiteTheWord29."

Thumb typing on his screen, I said, "Look for a game request."

With a couple of final taps, I sent a second stream of material into the diagram. The construct interpreted the input as new case information and created a second panel for the photos. The images arranged themselves one at a time, building a diagram of the second murder scene.

Remi's office reflected the personality of its occupant. Elegant. Contained. Efficient and neat.

The Barbgazi didn't die at his desk. The body lay sprawled face down in front of a chair typically reserved for visitors. He'd been sitting with his back to the door. Bad idea.

"Could you tell what Remi was working on?" I asked.

Press pointed to the scattered pieces of paper under the corpse. "Wine pairings for tonight's dinner. Those documents are menu specials from the chef."

My eyes moved back and forth comparing the two crime scenes.

Short man. Sitting back to the door. Convenient fire ax. Longer handle than the hatchet. Better control. The angle of the blow looked identical, though.

When Remi fell forward, he turned over a glass of red wine that had apparently been perched on the edge of his desk. The stain pooled with the blood on the beige carpet.

My attention skittered to a halt at the victim's right hand. "Are those scratches?"

Press nodded and watched as my fingers danced in the air, manipulating the diagram. I copied the new photo, zooming in on the back of Remi's hand, and arranged the image beside two others—the dresser from the Reynolds's room and the back of Frank's neck.

"Those marks are the same in all three places," I said.

Squinting, Press said, "Not quite, but close. The scratches on Remi's hand look almost tentative. What the hell is going on out there and why was Frank Reynolds carrying *this*?"

He held up the bottle containing the diamond. Somehow we'd neglected to discuss that big, shiny elephant in the drain. That's when I realized Press and I hadn't had a chance to discuss *anything* about the case since the previous day. We didn't have one elephant on our hands, we had a whole *herd*.

"I'm so sorry, Press," I apologized. "No sleep and finding out about Remi's has me all scattered. I didn't mean to do it, but you're out of the loop on several new bits of information."

Truthfully, I was used to withholding information from the vampire, not sharing with him, which I think Press knew but was nice enough not to mention. He gestured at the diagram. "Does that thing come with a whiteboard?"

With a few taps on the phone and a word or two of Latin, I produced the board and a set of colored markers. He looked like he wanted to laugh. "I'm not a color-coordinated kind of guy, Mattie. Black will do. You talk, I'll write."

I started with Frank popping into the Dodge the morning before when I left the police station and ended with seeing Frank and Vanessa enter the lodge's lobby roughly an hour before Remi died.

The detective's eyes narrowed. "Well, I don't like the sound of *that*. Okay. Do we have everything now?"

In a surprisingly neat hand, Press recorded the facts I shared, incorporating other key points of the investigation as he went in a highly efficient procedural shorthand.

Frank Reynolds
- killed with hatchet
- carrying a diamond(s)
- scratches on back of neck
- same as scratches in the room?
- ice bucket and scoop missing
- purple stain on shoe sole

Floyd Reynolds
- having affair with brother's wife
- carrying uncirculated $500 bills
- completed Frank's "deal" in town?
- sold diamonds? who was buyer?

Vanessa Reynolds
- unfaithful, possibly gold digger?
- said Floyd wouldn't kill brother on purpose
- discovered husband's body

Remi
- discovered credit card fraud
- someone watching him?
- was he protecting innocent party?
- killed with ax? copycat? same killer?
- scratches on back of hand
Buckshot
- wants credit card angle squelched
- may have brought rescue werewolf to town
- same person Remi protecting?
- involved in credit card fraud?

"Wow," I said. "You're good at this."

He gave me a bemused look. "I've had decades of practice. Are we on the same page now?"

"Yes, I think that's everything."

To my surprise and pleasure, he said, "You're good at this, too. That's a lot of useful information to turn up in 24 hours."

"Thank you. What's our next move?"

He capped the marker. "Santos has already removed Remi's body and put a rush on the autopsy."

That confused me. "Why a rush?"

"Barbgazi custom. We have to bury Remi before sundown today. The Joneses have offered a spot on their land up on the mountain. Before we can do anything else, we have a funeral to plan."

Chapter 22

PRESS WASTED NO TIME getting on the horn to Jerry. He instructed his partner to make sure Floyd and Vanessa didn't leave town. As I went out the back door, I heard the vampire say, "If they give you any trouble, arrest them on suspicion of murder."

We still weren't sure if either of them had killed Frank or Remi, but holding the pair in temporary custody would give us another 24 hours to make that determination if circumstances forced us down that path.

Of course, that strategy would also push Buckshot right over the cliff. He would lose his mind if Press started arresting paying visitors. People who get put in jail during their destination vacation don't leave good Yelp reviews.

But then the mayor had some explaining of his own to do.

By now it was almost 8 o'clock. Uncle Grim would be up. I climbed the external stairs to his apartment over the garage and knocked. He answered immediately. "Come on in."

I found my uncle sitting in his easy chair by the window, Sunday paper open in his lap. When I broke the news about Remi, Grim lowered his head. "That's a crying damn shame. Remi was good people. What can I do to help?"

"Press and I are going to drive over to Raylene's and get her working on the funeral details. While she's doing that, we have to check in with Santos and then go out to the Lodge so I can see the crime scene for myself."

My uncle eyed me closely. "Are you sure you want to do that? This isn't like some stranger's ghost showing up on the doorstep needing help. Remi was your friend."

Tears filled my eyes, but I didn't let them fall. "Which means I owe it to him to bring his murderer to justice."

Grim nodded. "I can understand that. You tell Raylene to call me. I'll get the boys together and we'll do whatever she needs."

"Thank you. That's sweet, and if I know Raylene, she'll put you all to work. Actually, I'm here to ask about the boys. Were you all able to figure out where Floyd Reynolds might have gotten those $500 bills?"

"Maybe," Grim said evasively, "but the feller we have in mind is mighty private. Some of us were going to try and talk to him this afternoon if he'll let us in."

I had no idea who in town Grim might be talking about, but I trusted my uncle to work that angle on his own. "Good. Call me if you find out anything you think I need to know."

When I came down to the driveway, Press was already seated behind the wheel of the Plymouth Model 30-U that was his private car. The Miller's Cove police department uses a fleet of 1940 Ford coupes with a single bubble light on the roof.

The first time I saw Press in the green Plymouth, I snooped a bit and discovered he'd driven the car back from Chicago when he came home to Miller's Cove. Since then, the vampire has lovingly maintained the car, happily bringing it out of mothballs for the town's new retro look.

The day hadn't gotten warm yet, but I knew Press's car had no air conditioning. "Are you sure you don't want to take my Dodge?" I asked.

The vampire grinned. "Are you sure you want your neighbors to see my car parked in your driveway all day?"

I got in the Plymouth.

Gossip flies at the speed of imagination in a small town and every made-up story gets more outrageous per telling. The news that Press and I were working together had probably already hit the local gossip mill, with speculations about our potential couple status soon to follow. The match had been struck; we didn't need to fan the flames.

On the way to Raylene's, Press said, "You use dead moonshiners and hexed flower vases a lot in your investigations?"

And here I thought we'd avoided this conversation altogether. "Using Aqua Netta was Raylene's idea. As for Shifty, he gets the job done, and he works cheap."

"How cheap?"

My response wasn't going to go over well. "Five minutes of sufficient corporeality to drink a Mason jar of shine."

Press's hands tightened on the wheel. "Where do you get..."

"Don't ask me that question," I warned. "I won't tell you, and I don't want us to start fighting again. Shifty's already dead. Illegal liquor isn't going to do him any harm."

The vampire's jaw set. "I'm worried about the living people who drink that swill. The last thing we need is a rampant run of jake leg in this town."

I couldn't contain my laughter. "Press, really? *The jake leg?*"

He was referring to partial paralysis of the legs and feet caused from drinking poisonous bootleg whiskey. Oklahoma City had the distinction of being the first municipality to experience an epidemic of the boozy plague in 1930. Several concoctions were to blame for the malady, including an 80 proof product marked as a "flavor extract"—Jamaican ginger extract—referred to as "jake" in slang.

Press wasn't amused. "I was in Chicago when bootlegging was the underpinning of organized crime. You don't want to know what a Tommy gun can do to a man's body."

"So that's why you called the revenuers on Shifty."

"I like a drink as well as the next man, Mattie, but the legal kind."

"Shifty is *dead.* The still blew up and killed him. No one can't drink moonshine made of ectoplasm, not even a ghost."

He didn't take his eyes off the road. "But you know someone who makes the real thing."

"You're thinking about the old timers who aged their whiskey with car batteries."

"I'm thinking about the major dangers of home distilling: lead poisoning and methanol toxicity. Which is why the practice is still illegal."

Arguing with him was easier when I thought he had his head in the past, not the science.

"That's true," I admitted, "but the person making the shine I give to Shifty uses a copper still that gets sterilized between every batch. We're talking organic, GMO-free crushed corn and imported artisan barley. It's a hobby for private consumption. Every now and then I get a jar to pay Shifty. That's all. I'm not going to get a friend in trouble for a hobby."

The vampire drew in a deep breath. "Please tell me you don't drink that stuff."

At that, I finally clued in. Press worried I might be drinking dangerous home-made whiskey. He didn't know how to express his concern, so he shifted to default mode: grumpy cop.

"I don't drink shine."

"And it's not Grim or Raylene running the still."

"It's not Grim or Raylene."

Press's hands finally relaxed on the steering wheel. "Good, because I don't think this relationship would have a chance if I started arresting your friends and family."

Thank sweet Hecate he said that as he pulled into Raylene's driveway. I had no idea how to respond to his statement about our "relationship" having a chance.

Did he mean our professional relationship? Or our friendship? Or another kind of relationship? That much confusion I didn't need. We were on much firmer footing with one another when we kept to the topic of murder.

I got out of the Plymouth fast before the vampire could ask more questions or say something else that would leave me stumped and flustered. As I strode up the walk, I heard Press get out of the car and follow me.

Raylene answered the door wearing a silk kimono with her hair tied up in a scarf. "Mattie, what are you doing here this early?" Then she caught sight of Press over my shoulder. "What's happened?"

There was no good way to break the news, so I just told her. "Oh, no," Raylene said, standing back to let us in. "Not Remi. You have to find out who did this to him."

"We plan to," I said, tight-lipped, "but we need your help with something. Press says that Barbgazi custom requires the dead be buried before the next sundown from the time of their passing."

She glanced at her wristwatch. "Which gives us about 12 hours."

"Santos is putting a rush on the autopsy," Press explained. "Mattie and I are on our way there now. The Joneses are supplying a gravesite and the reception will be at the barn, but I don't know about all the other details like..."

Raylene stopped him. "Leave all of that to me. Tell Santos to send the body to the Jenkins Mortuary. I do Jenny Belle's hair, so Homer won't argue about getting everything done today. Do you know how the Barbgazi feel about embalming?"

Press gave her a helpless look.

"Never mind," Raylene said crisply. "I'll get Marlene to let me in the special reading room at the library. We'll research the culture and make sure everything's done the right way."

Our local library has a basement collection of paranormal reference and reading material that we keep strictly away from the tourists.

The three of us briefly discussed potential pallbearers and how to activate the emergency funeral-food phone chain before Raylene shooed us to the door. Press went first, but Raylene pulled me into a big hug. "How are you, sugar?"

"Keeping it together, but I can't stop thinking that if we'd followed Floyd and Vanessa into the lobby last night Remi might still be alive."

"That's what I figured," she said, holding me at arm's length. "Do not do that to yourself. You don't know that Floyd and Vanessa are responsible for Remi's death. If we'd followed them inside last night, *we* might be the ones laid out on Santos's table this morning."

When I gave her a blank, deer-in-the-headlights look, she sighed and said, "You never think about that kind of thing, do you, Mattie? There's a killer loose out at the Lodge. Promise me that you'll be careful."

I gave her my word and went out to join Press who was leaning against the hood of the Plymouth smoking a Lucky. When he saw me coming, he put out the cigarette and dropped the butt in his pocket rather than litter Raylene's yard.

That courtesy didn't stop me from paying him back for the grilling about the moonshine, but my attempted lecture was dead on arrival when I started with, "Those things are going to kill you."

Press, who had opened the passenger side door like the gentleman he is, looked at me like I'd said the stupidest thing on earth—which I had. The fact that my face had already gone beet red saved him from actually *telling* me the statement was stupid.

"Let me rephrase that," I said as I climbed into the car. "Those things are going to kill the people who have to inhale your secondhand smoke."

"Okay," he chuckled, "I guess I deserve that. I'll try to confine my smoking to the company of folks who have already kicked the bucket. Good enough?"

"No," I said sourly, "but it's a start."

Most Sunday mornings I love to drive around Miller's Cove. We may be paranormal, but we're not heathens. Some of our denominations look like yours and some don't, but the point is that we stop once a week and spend some time thinking about the things in the Universe that are bigger than our individual concerns.

Afterward, there's a mad dash to find a parking space at the two or three local eateries the tourists don't frequent. For the rest of the afternoon in the warm months, you can find people mowing their lawns, barbecuing in the backyard, playing ball with the kids, or napping on their front porches.

That Sunday, the sunlight didn't seem so bright or the waves of the townspeople as animated. Word had gotten out about Remi's death and was spreading fast. The Barbgazi had been a beloved member of the community. His funeral would draw genuine mourners.

Press parked in front of the police station and cut the engine. "You could wait in my office while I get the autopsy report from Santos," he offered.

"I appreciate that, but no thank you," I said. "I've seen bodies on autopsy tables before."

"This is different."

As if I could forget that part with everyone I know reminding me every five minutes.

"Yes, but I need to get a look at those scratches on Remi's hand for myself."

The vampire's brow furrowed. "With all the other evidence, why are you fixated on those scratches?"

"They're the one common denominator in the two murders and they were present in Frank and Vanessa's room."

"Both men were killed by a single blow to the head from a blade. That's a common denominator."

"The assailant used a hatchet with Frank and an ax with Remi."

"Yes, but the switch in weapon could be nothing more than a matter of opportunity. The ax was right there outside Remi's office, and the perp had already killed that way once."

Only one person could tell us how similar—or dissimilar— the two murders really were—the witch doctor who examined both head wounds.

Chapter 23

THE SOUND OF SLOW DRUMBEATS drew us down the hall to Santos's lab. When Press opened the door, a cloud of smoke sent me retreating against the far wall with my hand over my mouth.

"Has he set the lab on fire?" I coughed.

Obviously respiratory issues don't trouble Press. "No. He's conducting one of his more spiritual autopsies. Push through. It will be better on the other side."

I took several quick breaths of relatively clean air and forged forward. When I emerged through the thickest smoke, I expected to see a tribal circle dancing around Remi's body, but the drums came from a record on the Zenith turntable next to Santos's desk.

The witch doctor had placed standing censers at either end of the metal table that held the corpse. Wearing a lab coat and feathered headdress, Santos stood beside Remi's sheet-draped form chanting softly in rhythm with the gourd rattle in his hand.

We stayed back and waited until he finished. When Santos opened his eyes, the pupils burned bright yellow before slowly fading back to brown when he focused on Press. "Hello, bloodsucker."

With a completely deadpan expression, Press said, "Morning, Dr. Nose Bone."

The insults covered the feelings with which both men struggled. Santos cleared his throat and nodded at Remi. "I don't know his tradition, but I've been trying to keep his soul at peace until he makes the crossing to the other side."

Then, as if noticing me for the first time, he added, "Hi, Mattie."

Fighting not to get choked up again, I said, "Hey, Santos. Thank you for taking such good care of him."

The witch doctor took off his headdress and put it on a nearby pedestal reserved for that purpose.

Absent his ceremonial gear, Santos reverted to his role as medical examiner. "All we can do with an end like Remi's is to listen to what the dead try to tell us about their fate."

The Barbgazi's body had a good bit to say compared to the information Santos gleaned from Frank Reynolds's corpse. Both men died of blows to the head delivered by a right-handed assailant, but whereas the strike to Frank's skull showed signs of hesitation, a deliberate, well-aimed cut killed Remi.

Since Frank had been kneeling and Remi sitting, the Barbgazi's smaller stature made the two targets of roughly equal height. Calculating relative force and angle of entry, Santos felt both victims could have been killed by the same person.

"How sure are you about that?" Press asked.

"Maybe 95%."

The number didn't satisfy the detective. "That 5% could land us in a lot of hot water if we arrest the wrong person. What else do you have for us?"

"Look at this," Santos said, leading us to a table where Remi's clothes were laid out. The witch doctor picked up a light wand and passed the beam over the black fabric. The illumination revealed a network of fine hairs. "Something shed all over the carpet in Remi's office. When he fell forward, the fibers covered his clothing."

Press made an irritated sound, one with which I was all too familiar. "Come on, Santos! Some*thing*? Surely you can do better than that."

Crossing his arms, Santos said, "Fine, but this could land us in hot water *and* bite us in the backside. The fibers look like werewolf hair to me."

The vampire scrubbed at his face and let loose with some pointedly profane remarks. "Great. Just freaking *great*. That means we have to have a conversation with the mayor. On a *Sunday*. Less than a week before the full moon. When he's already said he wants the trouble at the Lodge to go away fast."

Santos grinned. "I can whip up a protection potion for you if you can find me the inner eyelids of six Peruvian fruit bats."

Press glowered at him. *"Pass.*

"Well, I can tell you that there were no werewolf hairs on Frank Reynolds. I double checked."

From the look on the detective's face, I could tell that he did not regard the information as helpful in the slightest. Time for me to enter the conversation.

"Buckshot said he wanted the *credit card* trouble to go away fast," I said. "He doesn't have any justification to sweep two murders under the rug. Santos, have you had any luck identifying the purple gunk on the bottom of Frank's shoe?"

"No. The DNA results won't be back until tomorrow morning."

With the science out of the way or on hold, we told Santos that Raylene had taken on the funeral arrangements and would send Homer Jenkins to pick up the body.

"I'll call Homer and tell him to come ahead now," Santos said. "Unless you have any objections, Press."

"No, that's fine. Go ahead. Mattie and I were on our way to the Nostalgia Nook, but I guess we have to pay a call on the mayor first."

We walked back to the Plymouth in silence. On the way, I committed a cardinal sin of investigation; I let myself think we'd had all the curve balls that could come our way in one morning.

Big mistake.

When I halted in my tracks at the top of the station steps, Press said, "Now what?"

"Frank Reynolds is sitting in your car."

The vampire squinted toward the Plymouth. "I see that."

Wait. What? "You can see him?"

"I can," Press affirmed, "which I hope means he's ready to answer some questions without you acting as his interpreter. When did you last see the guy, anyway?"

"When he appeared in the backseat after Raylene and I left the barn and were on our way to the Lodge. He had good energy when he showed up, but faded fast."

Frank, who had been watching the sparse traffic on Main Street, spotted us and waved.

I answered the gesture, disguising the move at the end by smoothing my hair just in case any outsiders were out and about.

As we started down the steps, Press said, "Isn't he unusually unstable for a ghost?"

"Cut him some slack. He has a hatchet stuck in his head."

Press looked closer and had to stifle a laugh. "He's been wandering around this hole time with a ghost ax in his skull? How do you keep a straight face when you talk to him?"

"Trade secret," I said. "Now hush."

When Press and I got in the car, Frank immediately said, "The little man with the big feet from the restaurant is dead, isn't he?"

I experienced a split second of cold dread. "You haven't seen him, have you?"

"No," Frank replied. "I haven't seen anyone like me. The people at the Lodge are talking about it."

Thank, Hecate. I couldn't stand the thought of Remi caught between worlds. Santos had said his spirit was still on this plane waiting to cross over, but that's not the same as the condition in which Frank found himself. The Barbgazi custom of a sunset burial suggested to me that lingering for a few hours was nothing more than a part of how their kind negotiated the transition.

"Have you been at the Lodge since I saw you last night?" I asked Frank.

The spirit looked confused. "I don't always know where I am or what time it's supposed to be, but I like to stay close to Vanessa if I can."

Press and I exchanged a sidelong glance. Neither one of us thought Vanessa had a chance in hell at making Wife of the Year, no matter how devoted her poor sap of a husband continued to be.

Twisting in the driver's seat to get a better look at the ghost, Press said, "It's nice to meet you in person, Frank. Do you feel like answering a few questions?"

"Yes, but can we go somewhere with people? I like to watch people. It makes me feel not so dead."

I winced. Frank was developing a serious case of life longing, another symptom of a spirit well on his way to becoming a permanent haunt.

Press deferred to me. "Suggestions?"

"Swing by the Deja Vu. I'll ask Rosie to make us some sandwiches and we can take them to the park. We might as well have brunch before we confront Buckshot."

Eating to mask our feelings seemed to be the theme of the day.

Frank perked up when I mentioned the mayor. "That's the man who doesn't like to discuss outhouses. He adopts strays. I don't think he's done anything wrong."

Please, dear Goddess, let Frank be right.

We beat the lunch crowd at the diner. Rosie outdid herself, handing an old-fashioned wicker picnic basket over the counter to me. "I am *thrilled* to death about you and Press, sweetheart, He's needed a good woman in his life since FDR got elected. You all have fun now."

See what I mean about the speed of gossip? If NASA could have harnessed that power for rocket fuel, man would have reached the moon a decade earlier.

Press chose one of my favorite spots at the park without prompting—a grassy patch at the base of an oak next to the arched bridge over the pond. I hoped he liked it for its romantic appeal, but I suspected the deep shade had a great deal to do with the selection.

The vampire produced a plaid blanket from the Plymouth's trunk and spread it over the turf. While I unpacked the basket, which included actual plates strapped to the lid, Frank arranged himself at the base of the tree.

"Look at all of them outside enjoying the sunshine," he said wistfully. "I don't think I ever took Vanessa for a walk in the park."

A cartoonish image of Vanessa trying to walk on a lawn in stilettos formed in my mind. *I'd* take her to the park to enjoy that visual treat.

Press accepted a roast beef sandwich with a side of chips and a soda. I made my plate and gave him a pointed look.

"What?" he mouthed.

I jerked my head toward the ghost. *"Ask questions."*

"You start."

That got the vampire an even more emphatic impression of a mime. *"Press!"*

Sighing in resignation, he said, "Frank, can we talk about your business affairs?"

A doubtful ripple passed through the ghost. "I don't remember much."

The detective tried a more direct line of inquiry. "Do you remember anything about diamonds?"

Frank's eyes followed a laughing little girl throwing a ball for her puppy. "There were six, but I dropped them. They might still be there."

Press and I stilled. "Did you come to Miller's Cove to sell the diamonds?" I asked.

The spirit shimmered again. "I didn't steal anything, but I should have told him. That part wasn't right. Is that why I'm dead?"

Neither Press nor I could answer that. Frank stood abruptly and started across the bridge, disappearing at the midpoint.

"He's doing that more often," I said. "If we don't get to the bottom of this business soon, we're going to lose him."

Press took a bite out of his sandwich and chewed contemplatively. "So he brought legal diamonds to town to sell them for those $500 bills. Technically, that's not illegal."

"More like a 'buyer beware' situation," I agreed. "Frank knew he was getting something of greater value in the exchange, but he didn't tell the buyer."

"Right, so if Grim finds out the identity of that person, we might make that part of this mess right."

Finally, a few pieces of the puzzle inched together. "Floyd found the other five stones and completed the deal with the buyer."

"But Floyd didn't know the actual value of the bills either, so we can't make a fraud charge stick. Especially when Vanessa could very convincingly plead ignorance."

I almost choked on a chip. "Press! That wasn't very nice."

He paused with his soda bottle half-way to his mouth. "Please, make a case for her intellectual brilliance. I'd love to hear it."

"Fine. Can we put the screws to Floyd for stealing the diamonds from his brother?"

"Doubtful. The rocks technically belong to Vanessa, too. If she gave them to her brother-in-law, there's no crime. At most, we might get one or both of them for tampering with evidence."

Press was right. We couldn't connect the dots from possession of the diamonds to an ax in Frank's head.

I'll admit we lingered in the park longer than we should have. Neither one of us wanted to deal with Buckshot. If I could have chosen the outcome of that Sunday, I would have lounged in the warm air talking with Press for the rest of the day. Even if I couldn't see his eyes under those ever-present shades, I could tell the vampire was enjoying himself, too.

But, in the way of all picnics, we soon had nothing left but crumbs and the threat of ants. The last fragments on the blanket came from a dozen chocolate chip cookies Rosie thoughtfully tucked in the basket.

"We can't put this off any longer," Press said, brushing off his trousers with his napkin.

"What time is it?" I asked.

"Almost 1 o'clock."

Had we really killed an entire morning? As I repacked the basket and helped Press fold the blanket, I devoutly hoped Buckshot had enjoyed his Sunday meal.

Dealing with a werewolf suffering from a double homicide in his jurisdiction and heartburn appears exactly *nowhere* on my Sunday hit parade of good ideas.

Chapter 24

THAT OUTHOUSE INCIDENT isn't the only thing Hank "Buckshot" Leonard doesn't like to discuss. Under normal circumstances, he's not keen on delving into the details of his divorce either. The former Mrs. Mayor had many things in common with her husband, but turning furry on the full moon wasn't among them.

There's no werewolf marriage law set in stone, but most shifters avoid mixed relationships as a practical matter. Werewolves feel the effects of the changing moon for a full week. Always territorial and given to mercurial moods, even the most well-mannered wolf gets nervous and snappish for those seven days. Another wolf gets that, growls back, and moves on.

Press and I were more than aware we would be catching Buckshot in the waxing phase of his moon fever. Translation: his mood could be getting worse by the second.

The mayor lives in a rambling ranch style home on the edge of town. The rear line of the property backs up to the woods so he's free to take the long, rambling walks that are a favorite pastime of his kind. I've never actually seen His Honor sniff the underbrush or lift his leg, but there are stories.

Press parked the Plymouth in the mayor's driveway. When we stepped out, the growl of a lawnmower engine guided us to the town's chief executive in the backyard. I assumed Buckshot had changed out of his good Sunday clothes in favor of work boots, worn jeans, and a faded blue shirt, but I would soon learn that wasn't the case.

We found him walking behind a cranky old push mower, concentrating on making perfectly straight, well-groomed lines in his carpet grass. I wondered if Buckshot spent that much time manicuring the lawn during his marriage. If so, that could have been a contributing factor to the divorce as well. Most women don't like to play second fiddle to yard work.

The mayor didn't see us until he realigned the mower for a pass in our direction. He acknowledged our presence with a wave, held up five fingers, which we took to mean "give me five minutes," and pointed to a collection of chairs on the patio.

We nodded, which prompted Buckshot to mime taking a drink. More gesticulations made us understand that we were to help ourselves to the contents of the cooler sitting on the back step. The Zen of the Lawn Mower seemed to have lulled Buckshot into a better frame of mind than we'd feared.

Press removed a couple of sodas from the cooler, popped the caps, and handed me a cold bottle. We each claimed an Adirondack chair and watched the mayor finish his job.

When he finally cut the engine, Buckshot took the time to stow the mower under a nearby shed before coming toward us, wiping the sweat from his brow with a red bandana.

"Thanks for waiting, you all," he called out. "Getting to be that time of the month for me. I don't like to go howling in the woods unless everything's in ship shape around the house. What's up?"

That's when we realized that Buckshot had been home all day. He hadn't gone to church and apparently no one had called to tell him about Remi's death—or if they had the mayor hadn't heard the phone over the sound of the lawn mower. The grim task of breaking the bad news fell to us.

I guess Buckshot absorbed the information as well as could be expected. Sitting forward in his chair, forearms resting on his knees, the mayor asked tightly, "Do you have a suspect?"

Press didn't beat around the bush. "We're not sure, but we found werewolf hair all over the carpet in Remi's office."

To my great relief, the mayor didn't make us drag the story out of him. "That would belong to Shawn, I imagine," he said. "Boy sheds like all git out whether he's shifted or not. Reckon I have a story to tell you all, but before I do, I'm sorry I yelled at you in your office, Press and I apologize for my rudeness to you in the lobby, Mattie."

"We're good," Press assured him.

"Us, too," I said. "Who is this Shawn person? Do you think he killed Remi?"

Buckshot sat up in his chair, leaned toward the cooler, and took out a cold beer. "I sure hope he didn't," he said, tilting the bottle back and taking a long pull. "But the whole situation with Shawn has been weighing on my conscience for weeks. We might as well start at the beginning. Have you ever heard of the WPL?"

As we listened, the mayor described how lucky he felt to have grown up in Miller's Cove as a shifter. In a paranormal community, he and the other werewolves in town didn't feel the unrelenting pressure to hide their true selves like wolves in the outside world.

"I became pack alpha without having to fight my way to the top," he explained. "We have a nominating process. Out there," he gestured vaguely toward the highway which led past the mountains toward purely human society, "I might have had to kill someone to get the job. Far as I can tell, there's not a job on this good earth I want bad enough to commit murder over, even in pack-sanctioned, one-to-one combat."

Had he married another shifter, Buckshot's life would have been far easier, but he fell in love with a half-elf/half human woman he met in Nashville. "Vickie never could come to peace with where she belonged in the world," he said sadly. "I wanted to have kids, but she was too afraid they'd turn out like me. That kind of bigoted talk eats at a man over time. When she finally left, I didn't have the energy or the desire to go after her. She sent the divorce papers by FedEx with a pre-paid return envelope. I just signed them and sent them back."

Okey dokey, then. Vanessa Reynolds wasn't the only candidate for Less Than Ideal Spouse of the decade.

Being newly single did not cure Buckshot of his desire for children, however. He has his name in with several adoption agencies that work with paranormals, but in the meantime he volunteers with the Werewolf Protection League to work out his parental urges.

"Most of the time I've served as a WPL big brother," he said. "I run up to Nashville a couple of times a week to spend time with my kids. You know, take them to a ballgame, get something to eat, talk about what it means to be a shifter in the modern world. Then I met Shawn Pruitt."

The then 17-year-old wolf had been living on the streets before he stumbled into the Nashville WPL headquarters. "He fell in with a bunch of thug street shifters," Buckshot said with disdain. "Losers that call themselves the Rabid Renegades. They're into drugs, which I am here to tell you do not mix well with moon fever. Petty theft pays for their supply, but I've heard rumors that the older members are branching out into more sophisticated schemes."

Orphaned at twelve, Shawn had known a better life when his parents were alive, and came to WPL to try to get away from the dead end the Renegades represented. "We hit it off," Buckshot said. "I...well, I forged his papers to let him move to Miller's Cove and got him a job at the Nostalgia Nook."

"Why did you fake his application?" I asked. "Didn't you think the admission committee would let him in?"

"No, because Shawn failed his last WPL drug test. It was just weed, but that would be enough to bar him from coming to Miller's Cove."

Beside me, Press shifted in his chair. "I hate to be the one to say this, Buck, but you wrote the zero tolerance policy on drugs for new residents."

"Don't remind me," the mayor said miserably. "Shawn swore to me he'd never smoke pot again, and he hasn't. I test him myself every week."

"Well, okay," Press said. "I guess that's fair enough, but it doesn't cover the credit card business. Remi talked with Mattie last night at the barn dance. He knew about the fraud and wanted an immunity deal for an innocent party in exchange for testimony. Do you think that person could be Shawn?"

Buckshot toyed with his now empty beer bottle. "No. I think it's more likely that Shawn is in the credit card thing up to his neck. The people at WPL warned me how hard it can be to get someone out of the Renegades, and Shawn is good with computers. I don't know how he's stealing the credit card information from the guests, but he'd certainly know what to do with the numbers and how to hide his tracks."

"If you believe he's guilty, why would you try to get Press to stop the investigation?" I asked.

The mayor heaved a weary sigh. "I didn't want anyone to know what an idiot I was bringing the kid to town. It's three days to the full moon. I intended to put the question to the pack."

The horror I felt must have registered on my face, because Buckshot hastened to reassure me. "No, no. It's not what you think. We wouldn't have killed him. We'd have expelled him from the pack and gotten him back to Nashville on the first bus out of town. If a werewolf gets kicked out of the local pack, he has no choice but to leave and look for a new home, which for Shawn would mean a return to the Renegades. Pack expulsion has been the law of our kind for centuries. We're not built to survive all alone. Executions are extremely rare and only used with the hardest of hard cases."

"Have you confronted Shawn about any of this?" Press asked.

"No."

"Do you know where he is now?"

"At work. I'm ashamed to admit this, but I took him to the vet and had him chipped so I could keep an eye on him."

Now come on. Stop already with the protests. How many parents have wanted to do that to their kids but kept quiet about it?

"What does Shawn do at the Lodge?" I asked.

"He's a busboy," Buckshot replied. "Remi was his boss."

When Buckshot learned that Press and I were headed to the Nostalgia Nook anyway, he asked to come along. We all planned to attend Remi's service at sunset, and since most of the town would be there, the three of us might as well go together.

Considering that we had to stop at my house so I could change into a dark dress, and run by Press's place so the vampire could don his usual double-breasted attire, we didn't save any time. But that really wasn't the point. Buckshot wanted our company. He'd not only lost a friend, but a young man in whom he'd invested time and care had likely betrayed him.

Lump all that in with moon fever, and the mayor was not having a good day.

Jerry met us in the lobby when we arrived at the Nostalgia Nook. Press must have called his partner and warned him that we were on the way because the detective didn't react to the sight of the mayor beyond saying, "Hey, Buckshot."

"Hey, Jerry."

"Okay," Press said, "here's what we're going to do. First, Mattie wants to have a look at the second crime scene. Then we're going to speak with Shawn Pruitt. Do you have eyes on him?"

"Yep," Jerry said. "I put a man on the back entrance out of the kitchen and another in the service hallway. Kid's up to his neck helping with a restock of the pantry, so he's not onto us yet."

"What about Floyd and Vanessa?" I asked.

"They came down for the lunch buffet and then went back to her room. There's a third officer watching both doors. Where do you want to talk to the Pruitt kid?"

"Let's do it in Remi's office," Press suggested. "If he is the killer, he might not like sitting there looking at a chalk outline of a body on the carpet."

Chapter 25

BEHIND THE MORE PUBLIC-facing spaces, the Nostalgia Nook still hews to the retro standard. Maybe the management worries that guests would wander into parts of the hotel where they didn't belong, or maybe they've come to fully embrace working in the past. We wound through a warren of offices with glazed, opaque windows and vintage brass mail slots.

Remi had one of the better placements at the rear of the building, a corner room with a lone window that looked out over the mountains. It was the one concession to aesthetics in a space that was otherwise the living definition of functional

The Barbgazi used a wooden desk that could have belonged to a high school teacher with the low-backed wooden chair on rollers to match. He'd undoubtedly chosen to sit in one of the guest chairs the night he died for the padding. Remi had made the utilitarian environs his own by relieving the sparse setting with personalized decor.

An elegant set of leather accessories covered the top of the desk, carefully arranged at exact angles with one another. What I had taken for carpet in the crime scene photos was actually a beige rug covering a hideous linoleum floor.

Paintings of mountains covered the walls. A small sofa—the perfect size for a short man to take an afternoon nap—sat opposite the desk. To its right, a bookcase held leather-bound and modest objets d' art.

I walked behind the desk and studied the piles of papers without touching anything. Notes for menus. Clipped wine reviews. Employee reports. All very businesslike; nothing suspicious.

Press leaned against the doorframe watching me while Buckshot waited outside in the hall.

"Mind if I look in the desk drawers?" I asked.

"Go ahead."

The top drawer held a predictable collection of office tools: letter opener, ruler, scissors. The inset front tray contained paper clips, extra staples, an eraser, and rubber bands.

Manila folders filled two standard file drawers on the left and right. Stationery, ink bottles, and postage stamps occupied the middle drawer on the left. The right middle, however, gave me pause.

Noticing my reaction, Press said, "Did you find something?"

I took out a bottle of hydrogen peroxide, a tube of antibiotic cream, gauze, and a roll of tape. "Why would Remi need all this first aid stuff? Did he have some kind of injury?"

"If he had, Santos would have mentioned it."

Plucking a pencil from the cup beside the blotter, I moved trash around in the basket under the desk. "Huh. No cast off bandages in here."

"Maybe he kept those supplies on hand for the kitchen workers," Press suggested. "You can get burned in all kinds of ways working food prep."

"True," I said, running my fingers over the edge of the desk. The wood was scarred and dinged, but two holes right at the edge looked deep and fresh. Which could have been caused by anything, I told myself.

Finally I studied the outline of Remi's body marked on the rug. My mind's eye filled in the space with the memory of the Barbgazi's crumpled form. That visual would be seared in my mind for some time to come, I didn't need to reinforce the details. "Okay, I'm done. Let's meet Shawn."

Truthfully, I expected Jerry to usher in a juvenile delinquent with slicked back hair and a package of cigarettes rolled in the sleeve of his white t-shirt. Someone Marlon Brando or James Dean would have played in the movie version of this story.

What I saw was a scared young man with sandy hair and a splash of freckles across his cheeks trying to look surly and failing. As Press predicted, Shawn did not react well to the outline of the body. The instant he saw it, the young werewolf scooted as far away from the place where Remi died as possible.

But then things went from bad to worse. Shawn spotted Buckshot, who had taken up position along with Press on one side of the desk, the boy's lip trembled for an instant before he regained a thin semblance of self-control. Addressing the mayor, he said, "What are you doing here?"

Buckshot's nostrils flared, but he held his temper. "I'm here with Chief of Police Jackson and Miss Tucker. She's a private investigator looking into the death of the guest who was found at the ice machine on Friday."

"I don't know nothing about that."

"*Anything*," Buckshot said, growling low in his throat. "You don't know *anything*. Stop pretending to be ignorant and show some manners."

Understand that when I use the word "growl," I mean it in the most literal sense. Whatever else Shawn Pruitt might be, he was not an alpha wolf. The instant he heard that deep rumble from his pack leader, the boy's gaze dropped to the carpet and he said, "Yes, sir."

"That's better," the mayor said. "Get one thing straight here, Shawn. Chief Jackson can put you in jail, but *I* can turn you over to the pack."

By this time if Shawn's house breaking had failed him, I wouldn't have been surprised. He looked like a chastened puppy, and I was starting to feel sorry for the kid.

Buckshot hadn't moved a muscle. He didn't have to. With nothing but the timbre of his voice, the mayor clearly established himself as the big dog in the room.

Satisfied that he'd put Shawn in his place, Buckshot nodded at Press, who leaned against the wall and shoved his hands in his trouser pockets. I knew what he was doing, striking a casual, relaxed pose in contrast to the mayor's display of dominance.

"Hey, Shawn," Press said. "Mind telling us where you were last night?"

The boy's eyes darted between the two men. "In my room in the staff quarters."

I took his answer as polite enough, but Buckshot wasn't satisfied. At another growl from his mentor, Shawn almost jumped off the couch.

"*Sir,*" he said quickly. "I was in my room in the staff quarters, *sir.*"

"Relax," Press said, which could have been a directive to Shawn, the mayor, or both. "Can anyone verify that?"

"No, sir."

"Why did we find your hair all over this room?"

"Mr. D'Aboville was teaching me, sir. I came here so we could talk about my lessons."

"What kind of lessons?"

The boy looked close to tears. "Food and wine. Books and art. Stuff like that. He said I'd always be kitchen help in the hospitality industry If I didn't learn how to be a gentleman."

None of us expected that answer, but neither were we surprised. If Remi saw a way to give a young person like Shawn a leg up in the world, he would never fail to seize such an opportunity.

"Shawn," I said, "you liked Mr. D'Aboville, didn't you?"

The boy fidgeted and his voice broke when he answered , "Yes, ma'am. I did."

"How do you think he would have felt if he knew you'd been stealing credit card information from the guests here at the Lodge?"

A lone tear flowed down Shawn's face. "He was disappointed in me, ma'am."

"So he did know that you were behind the credit card fraud?"

"Yes, ma'am."

"Can you tell us about that?"

When Shawn looked uncertain, Buckshot gave him a stern warning, "Now is not the time to start lying, boy."

From the doorway, Jerry interrupted the interrogation. "I can save us some time. The Rabid Renegades put Shawn up to the whole thing. I have a buddy on the force in Nashville. He tells me the Renegades have been running this same scam in at least five hotels there. One of their members is a witch who worked out the hex to make the victims accept the fraudulent charges. You've been using the same magic here, haven't you, kid?"

The young werewolf nodded, but didn't look up.

"Okay," Press said, "here's the part we don't get. The Renegades are planting credit card skimmers in Nashville, but that won't work here because guests only use cards at check out and the Lodge prefers the old-fashioned carbon paper method to capture the charge information. The duplicatess are locked in the manager's safe immediately after each transaction. How have you been getting the numbers?"

I didn't now when Press and Jerry had time to coordinate coming at Shawn with the facts of the scam, but they were executing an effective one-two punch that left the boy no place to run.

Shawn's parents must have raised him right, or maybe some of Buckshot really had started to rub off on the young man. The kid was scared, but resolute. He found the courage to look Press in the eye and say, "I'm sorry, sir, but I can't tell you that part."

Buckshot's expression darkened, "You mean you *won't* tell us."

Now crying openly, Shawn said, "No, sir, I mean I can't. I did what the Renegades told me to do because they said they know where my little sister is and if I don't steal the numbers for them they'll hurt her. I'll take my punishment for the credit cards, but Mr. D'Aboville said we all have a responsibility to protect those who can't protect themselves and that's what I'm going to do."

The mayor looked like someone had hit him in the face. "Shawn, why didn't you tell me that you hav a sister?"

"When our parents died child protective services separated me and Susie. I hit the streets before they could put me in a foster home like they did her. The Renegades took me in."

Big-hearted pack of crooked cur dogs that they are. "If the Renegades took care of you why did you try to get away from them?" I asked.

"I didn't want to steal anything," Shawn said, "so I went to WPL. When Mr. Leonard offered me the chance to get out of Nashville, I took it, but the Renegades found me. They said I had the perfect job to be a contributing member of the gang and if I didn't Susie would pay for my disloyalty. Nobody can get away from the Renegades."

Press pushed off the wall, his eyes stormy with anger. "We'll see about that," he said, "but you're going to have to cooperate with us Shawn. How have you been collecting those credit card numbers?"

Sitting up straight, Shawn said, "No, sir. I'll tell you everything else, but not that."

While Jerry watched the kid, I stepped into the hall with Press and Buckshot. "He didn't kill Remi," I said.

"How can you be so sure?" Press asked.

"For starters, he's nothing but a scared child forced to grow up too fast. But more to the point, Shawn wears his wristwatch on the right side. He's left-handed. Santos said both vics were killed by a right-handed assailant."

"She's right," Buckshot said. "The boy's a southpaw. We have to help him, Press. Here I thought Shawn was a bad kid who conned me. Come to find out the Renegades victimized him."

"Don't worry about that," the vampire said. "Jerry and I are already coordinating with the Nashville police. They're raiding the Renegades' club house tonight. The credit card fraud is dead in the water, but we still need to know who was helping Shawn and why he insists on protecting that person or persons."

"Give me some time with him," Buckshot said. "I'll try to get him to come completely clean. I'm going to call the WPL director and start tracking Susie down. She's not on the League's books, which means CPS placed her with a non-shifter family. That has to be corrected."

We all turned at the sound of approaching footsteps. Punk Jones came around the corner, red-faced and panting. "Sorry to interrupt, Chief," he said. "But we've got trouble."

"What kind of trouble?" Press asked.

"Floyd and Vanessa Reynolds came out of their rooms with their bags packed. When we explained that you'd like for them to stay in town, Mr. Reynolds pitched a fit. He threw a punch at me, but I ducked and herded him back inside."

Buckshot covered his eyes with his hand. "How much more complicated can this day get?"

"Don't say that," I warned. "You're asking for trouble."

"Where are the Reynoldses now?" Press asked.

Punk didn't enjoy breaking the rest of the bad news. "We detained them in their hotel rooms. I put a man on each door. Mr. Reynolds was yelling about calling his lawyer, but I don't think that will be a problem."

Press gave him a suspicious look, "And why would that be, Officer Jones?"

Punk grinned. "You know how unreliable those telephone switchboard systems are, sir. It's the darndest thing, but every phone in the Lodge went out at the same time."

He should have said the *right* time—before Floyd Reynolds could place a call that would bring outsiders into Miller's Cove business.

Chapter 26

VAMPIRES DON'T NEED to blink; a physiological advantage that allowed Press to stand impassively through the fit Floyd Reynolds threw when the three of us went to his room.

Buckshot tried to be the diplomat in the group. "Mr. Reynolds, my name is Hank Leonard. I'm the mayor of Miller's Cove. Surely you can understand that Chief Jackson is only trying to catch the person who murdered your brother."

Either Frank didn't understand that he and Vanessa were under suspicion, or he thought stomping his foot and holding his breath would get him somewhere with Press. Don't get in a breath holding contest with a vampire. Just don't.

"How exactly does arresting me and my sister-in-law contribute to solving Frank's murder? It's...it's...it's just not *fair*," Floyd stuttered. As he spoke he glanced in the mirror and absently wiped a dob of hysterical spittle from the corner of his mouth.

I had to look away to keep from laughing. What Floyd really needed was to be given his binkie and put down for a nap.

"No one here is under arrest...yet," Press said.

Floyd wheeled and pointed an accusing finger at Punk who stood expressionless by the door. "If this isn't an arrest, then you need to discipline this rogue officer of yours immediately. I want to file a complaint for police brutality."

"Officer Jones?" Press said.

"Yes, Chief?"

"Did you put your hands on Mr. Jackson?"

"No, sir."

"Did you see anyone put their hands on him?"

"No, sir."

By this time Floyd was red-faced and breathing hard. "Then ask him what he did to the phones to keep me from calling my lawyer. He did something. I know he did."

"Officer Jones?"

"Yes, Chief?"

"Did you do anything to the telephones?"

"No, sir. The outage is affecting the entire town."

Slumping into a chair, Floyd said, "Which is what you people get for using all this antiquated junk to bilk the tourists."

How I kept a straight face over Press's next question, I'll never know. "Have you tried your cellular phone, Mr. Reynolds?"

"Of course I've tried my damned cell phone," Floyd huffed. "No signal. What do you have to say about that? Huh? What did you do, cut the lines?"

And clearly we have incomprehension over the word "cellular."

Buckshot held out his hands in placation. "We've had a lot of trouble with the cell tower. The phone company says they're working on it. Since everyone in town has a landline, it's usually not a problem."

"This is *unacceptable*," Floyd said. "I'll sue the Lodge. I'll sue the town. I'll sue every one of you. You just watch."

Still unflappable, Press said, "That's your right, Mr. Reynolds. I'm sure the sale of your brother's diamonds netted a sufficient profit for you to afford the legal fees."

Floyd's face went pale and the torrent of threats trickled down to a weak, "I have no idea what you're talking about."

Press reached into his suit pocket and brought out the diamond Shifty found now in an evidence bag. "This gemstone was found in the drain under the ice machine where your brother was murdered."

That single, glittering rock might as well have been a naked light bulb dangling over Floyd's head. "So, what?" he said. "Anyone could have dropped that."

Press took a seat at the foot of the bed nearest to Reynolds and rested his forearms on his knees. "Not a lot of people in Miller's Cove wander around with a 2 caret Grade D diamond in their pockets. We've looked into your brother's import business. He acquired a lot of six diamonds shortly before coming to town for the weekend."

Two things. First, the police can lie to suspects during an interrogation. Second, "looking into" Frank's business amounted to disjointed conversations with the dead man's ghost, but his brother didn't need to know that.

"I don't know anything about my brother's business," Floyd said. "I have affairs of my own that demand attention."

One of those being with his brother's wife.

"I'm sure you do," Press said. "What is your line of work, sir?"

Floyd shifted in his chair. "I'm in consulting."

"What is your area of expertise?"

"The facilitation of business negotiations."

That sounded like the kind of job specifically made up for the fake résumé of a man who dedicated his time to doing as little work as possible.

"Did you go into a shop called Tucker's Horology on Main Street yesterday morning?" Press asked.

"Yeah. So what? Place has a lot of junky old watches."

The vampire turned to me. "Miss Tucker, what was the retail value of the merchandise Mr. Reynolds considered for purchase?"

"Nine thousand seven hundred and ninety-five dollars," I said. "Before taxes."

"And how did Mr. Reynolds try to pay for that merchandise?"

Putting on my best concerned proprietor persona, I said, "In what appeared to be uncirculated $500 bills. Fortunately, my Uncle

Grimshaw dabbles in coin collecting. He knew the numismatic value of the currency exceeded the asking price of the two Rolex watches."

Floyd frowned. "New missus what?"

Without hesitation, Press went into dictionary mode, "Of or referring to coins, paper currency, and medals. I understand that even though Mr. Tucker kept you from incurring a considerable financial loss, you left the store angry and were still upset some time later when you entered the Bygone Beauty Salon to pick up your sister-in-law."

"How did you...," Floyd stopped. "*That creepy vase!* I knew it was looking at me! You had no right to put a camera on me."

Press swiveled back to me. "Miss Tucker, are you friends with the proprietress of the Bygone Beauty?"

"I am."

"To your knowledge, does she employ cameras to spy on her customers?"

"Raylene has no cameras in her shop," I assured him. Note that we were both careful to put our emphasis on *"cameras"* while skirting the potential of more metaphysical types of spying.

Now looking more and more like the cornered rat he was, Floyd said, "Well, there's still something off about that place."

Circling back to the collectible currency, Press said, "Where did you get those $500 bills?"

Reynolds snapped. "That's it. I'm not saying another word to you people until I can talk to my lawyer."

Press stood up and buttoned his jacket. "Of course, sir. Floyd Reynolds, you are under arrest for suspicion of murder in the death of Frank Reynolds. You have the right to..."

Thankfully Press had informed Buckshot that he intended to put Floyd under formal arrest or the mayor might have passed out on the spot. We listened while Press finished reciting Frank's rights and Punk put the suspect in cuffs. As he was being led away, the vampire made certain Reynolds saw us going into this sister-in-law's room.

"You leave her alone!" Floyd yelled, struggling against the hold Punk had on him. "Vanessa! *Vanessa!* Don't tell them anything!"

The widow Reynolds was sitting on the couch when we entered, twisting a Kleenex to shreds in her hands. I couldn't help but notice that Imogene did a beautiful job with her nails.

Vanessa heard her brother-in-law's voice retreating in the distance. Before any of us could speak, she said, "What's wrong with Floyd?"

Press didn't pull any punches. "He's under arrest for suspicion of murder in the death of your husband."

She gasped and brought her hand and a wad of tissue fragments to her mouth in a perfectly timed theatrical display. "But that's impossible! Floyd wasn't even in town when Frank was killed."

"We haven't been able to verify the exact time of your brother-in-law's arrival," Press said. "May we sit down?"

"Of course," she said, looking at me. "You were here the other day."

"I was," I said. "My name is Mattie Tucker. I'm working with Chief Jackson. And this is Mayor Hank Leonard."

Buckshot extended his hand. "I'm sorry for your loss, Mrs. Reynolds."

Vanessa blinked like she was having trouble keeping up with the cast of characters. "Uh, thank you. Why are *you* here?"

Taking the seat opposite her on the couch, Buckshot said, "I try to stay in close contact with Chief Jackson. I wanted to extend the condolences of our community to you and apologize that we're going to have to ask you to stay in town a little longer than you expected. You understand that we're trying to tie up all the loose ends in your husband's case and make sure we've apprehended his killer."

Buckshot and Press were playing a game of good cop/bad cop. Lean on Floyd, shower Vanessa with sympathy.

"But I just can't believe that Floyd would kill Frank on purpose," she said in a breathy voice. I could have been mistaken, but I swore she batted her eyelashes at Buckshot.

"Does that mean you think he would have killed his brother by accident?" Press asked.

Realizing what she'd said, Vanessa backpedaled so fast she almost pushed the sofa through the wall. "No, I, uh, I didn't say that right. I just can't believe Floyd would have killed Frank at all."

"I'm sure this has all been a terrible shock." Press murmured with faux empathy. "Were you aware that your husband had business dealings in Miller's Cove?"

Vanessa's eyes worked back and forth like a slot machine trying to land on a jackpot. "He might have mentioned something about that. Maybe. Possibly."

Out came the diamonds again. "Was he possibly selling diamonds?"

Her gaze locked on the glittering stone. "Where did you get that?"

"In the drain under the ice machine. Our investigation has determined that your husband came to town with six diamonds. Do you know what happened to the other five?"

"I think Floyd would want me to talk to someone about how I should answer that," she said. "Like maybe a lawyer or an attorney or someone legal."

"Those are the same things," Press said. He didn't smile, but I saw the quirk in the corner of his mouth. "Are you asking for legal counsel?"

"I guess."

"Then this conversation is over," Press said. "I'm not going to place you under formal arrest, Mrs. Reynolds, but I can detain you for the next 24 hours. Please don't leave this room."

Vanessa's eyes went wide. "But we have dinner reservations."

"The city will reimburse you for room service," Buckshot said smoothly. "As an act of condolence. I'm sure this business with the diamonds will be cleared up when we have a chance to talk with your brother-in-law at greater length."

"Where is Floyd?" Vanessa said. "Can I talk to him?"

"I'm afraid not," Press said. "He's on his way to jail. We'll be back to talk to you tomorrow."

As the three of us exited the room, I made eye contact with Vanessa. She looked like one of those bug-eyed goldfish who just realized her tank was leaking profusely.

Press waited until we were out of earshot. "Okay, now we let those two spend the night stewing in their own juices. Mattie, can you summon Frank's ghost?"

"Now hold on there!" Buckshot said. "I don't think we need to be waking the dead."

"He's already awake," I assured him. "Frank Reynolds showed up in the alley behind the shop the morning after his murder, asking for my help."

"Oh," the mayor said. "Well, why haven't you all just asked him to name his killer?"

"That hatchet did a number on his brain," Press said. "Poor guy doesn't remember what happened, and he's got a bad habit of fading in and out."

"Then why do you want Mattie to get in touch with him?"

The vampire grinned. "Because I don't want Floyd to get lonesome in that jail cell tonight."

I saw where he was going with this plan and I liked it.

"Give me a few minutes alone," I said. "Frank hasn't answered me before, but I'm willing to try. Keep everyone away from the area around the ice machine, okay?"

"No problem," Press said. "We'll be in the lobby when you're done."

I went to the vacant stretch of wall and stood by the drain. "Frank," I said, "I know you can hear me and I understand why you've been keeping to yourself, but we need your help with something. Please come talk to me."

It took three tries, but finally the air beside me shimmered into the murdered man's form. "Vanessa is stress eating," he said. "She ordered dinner with three desserts and no salad. She always gets a salad."

"One big meal won't hurt her," I assured him. "You know that we've arrested your brother?"

He nodded. "I saw."

"Do you know if he's the one who killed you?"

"I'm not sure."

"Would you be willing to go to his jail cell and talk to him tonight?"

Frank frowned. "Don't you think that might scare him? Living people aren't very receptive to talking to dead people."

Massive understatement. "We *want* you to scare him, Frank. Somebody took your diamonds. Your brother wound up with the payments for those rocks, and he's trying to take your wife. Don't you think he deserves being haunted by you for at least one night? It might be kinda fun."

The ghost thought about the idea. "He always wins."

"Then it's your turn to come out on top for a change. We need you to shake him up enough that he'll answer Chief Jackson's questions honestly tomorrow. By helping us, you'll be helping yourself, Frank. You don't belong here on the earthly plane any more."

Nodding slowly, Frank said, "I know I don't. Sometimes I think I hear voices asking me to come with them to some other place, and I kinda want to go, but I can't."

"If you do this, you should be able to find out if that other place is where you'd like to be from now on."

That did the trick. "Okay, I'll go see Frank. You're going to the funeral for the little man with the big feet, aren't you?"

Where did that come from? "Yes, we are."

"I'm sorry he's dead," the ghost said. "You should talk to his pet. I think it could help."

And just like that, he was gone. Why the heck do they *always* have to say something totally ambiguous and *then* disappear?

Chapter 27

"HIS *pet?*" Press said. "Frank said we should speak to Remi's *pet?* You mean like a dog or a cat?"

"I have no idea," I replied, "but we should check it out before we leave for the funeral. Frank may be vague, but he's put us on to some good leads."

We were sitting in the Nostalgia Nook lobby with Buckshot watching guests check out. The process went exactly as Remi had described. The clerk at the desk brought out one of the old-fashioned carbon paper credit card processing gizmos, which the guest approved and signed. No period incorrect electronics involved.

Jerry questioned the clerk and confirmed that all the processing materials including the carbon paper gadget went back in the safe after each transaction.

Following up on my suggestion, Press spoke with the manager about Remi's "pet." When the vampire rejoined us, he said, "Frank's scrambled again. Remi doesn't have a pet. He lived in one of the larger staff apartments at the back of the building. No animals allowed."

Except rescue werewolves hired to work as busboys who perpetrate in-house fraud.

"I don't care if pets are allowed or not," I said. "We should look at Remi's room."

Press held up a dangling set of keys. "Which would be why I got these from the manager."

Wise guy.

The three of us trouped into the lower regions of the Lodge and located Remi's tiny apartment, which for the most part mirrored the precision and order we'd seen in his office. The only exception was a card table holding a 10,000 piece jigsaw puzzle. The picture was a panorama of the Swiss alps.

Tears filled my eyes when I thought about the Barbgazi sitting there assembling the tiny pieces that would now remain incomplete. "We should put the puzzle in the grave with him," I blurted out. "It wouldn't be right for anyone to finish it now."

Press and Buckshot didn't argue or tell me that I was being a sentimental wreck. Instead, good guys that they are, the two men carefully broke apart finished chunks of the puzzle and lifted them intact into the box. The loose pieces went in on top. On the drive out to the Jones's place, Buck held the box carefully in his lap, steadying it with both hands.

We arrived when the sun still sat above the mountain ridge. Raylene walked out and met us at the car. "Hey, you all. We need two more pallbearers."

Both men readily agreed to take on the somber responsibility. Buckshot handed the puzzle to Raylene. She stared down at the picture on top of the box. "What's this?"

"Remi was working on that in his room, and I, well, I thought we should bury him with it," I said, fighting to keep my voice steady.

Raylene knows me better than anyone in the world. She embraced the crazy idea without question, handing the box back to Buckshot. "You all go on up to the barn and find Punk. He got here about half an hour ago. I put him in charge of the pallbearers. He'll make sure this gets in the casket with Remi."

Press and Buckshot started up the slope to the barn, speaking to the townspeople who stood around in knots of threes and fours. Raylene put her hands on my shoulders, "How you doing there, sugar?"

"Awful," I admitted, letting tears roll down my cheeks. "This shouldn't have happened."

Wrapping me in a big hug, Raylene said, "That's not up to you, Mattie. The Universe makes those decisions. Come on. We have to start up the mountain soon."

We walked arm-in-arm to the barn where the women of the LIbrary Guild fussed with the reception tables. "Marlene called them in," Raylene explained. "While she helped me look into Barbgazi funeral customs, the Guild ladies got to work on the food."

Raylene and Marlene discovered that the Barbgazi bury their dead in woven baskets so the body can return to the earth naturally. "Homer didn't have any biodegradable caskets," Raylene said, rearranging a stack of napkins. "He drove all the way up to Nashville to pick one up. There's an undertaker over there who does green funerals."

I looked out the open back door of the barn toward the mountain slope. A cloud of fairies hovered over a spot near the summit. "What are they doing up there?"

"Blasting out the grave with fairy dust," she said. "The ground's almost solid rock, but that's not a problem since we *need* the rocks. The Barbgazi erect stone cairns over their dead. The fairies are opening the grave and some of the werewolves are up there with them to stack the rocks. Those guys get awful strong this time of the month."

Across the room, I spotted Uncle Grim and some of the boys from the Guild. I excused myself and went over to them. All the men rose to their feet as I approached, each taking his turn at giving me a big hug.

"Did you all find out who might have had those $500 bills?" I asked, being careful to ensure that no one could overhear our conversation.

Not only had they identified the diamond buyer, they'd had a meeting with him. All small towns have figures who fulfill signature roles that, while not politically correct by modern standards, are also important filaments in the off-beat fabric of our lives.

For instance, we have a town drunk. He only gets liquored up two or three times a week, and he doesn't do anyone any harm.

Unfortunately, he has no interest in being the founding member of the Miller's Cove chapter of Alcoholics Anonymous. Which is a shame—for his health and for our nostalgic authenticity; AA started in 1935.

I did not know until that afternoon, however, that we also have a reclusive dragon shifter who lives, appropriately, in a stone cottage up at Fire Rock Gap. Mandrake Oliver stays away from other people because his kind suffer from uncontrollable heartburn.

No, not the kind caused by eating spicy food. Dragon shifters nurse an internal flame, which they vent with pyrotechnic bursts several times a day. In deference to the fire marshall's understandable concerns and his own preference for solitude, Mandrake lives alone and off to himself.

He makes his living writing a series of highly successful fantasy books, which feature dragons. The stories have been made into a blockbuster Hollywood trilogy, so Mandrake has no financial concerns.

Since he's so far outside the city limits, Mandrake's use of satellite Internet doesn't imperil the town's cultivated image. His refusal to interact with his fans has given him a kind of J.D. Salinger allure, but most of them believe that he lives in the Canadian wilderness.

Every now and then one of his devotees makes the news for almost becoming bear chow stomping around in the snow in search of their hero.

Beyond the fire component, dragon shifters have one other driving passion—the lust for treasure. Mandrake acquired the vintage $500 bills in 1945 after the government discontinued the denomination. He had a vague awareness that the currency had appreciated in value, but found the paper unsatisfying. Dragons like their treasure to sparkle and shine.

"Your murdered feller and Mandrake got together online," Grim said. "Frank Reynolds belonged to a treasure collectors discussion forum. He and Mandrake got to having private conversations. When Frank said he'd come into some diamonds, Mandrake offered to pay him with the paper money."

And Frank conveniently forgot to mention that he would be the one making a killing in the deal.

Since Mandrake doesn't like to interact with people, the two men arranged a drop at the base of the mountain the shifter calls home. Mandrake put the money in an old mailbox and watched from a distance while the man he assumed to be Frank Reynolds, exchanged the bills for a velvet bag holding the diamonds.

Mandrake had never seen his online friend, but even if he had, he couldn't have known that Frank had an identical twin. In a rare burst of honesty, Floyd had returned a few bills during the exchange along with a note explaining that he'd only been able to bring five diamonds.

I thanked Uncle Grim and the boys and started to find Press to tell him we had proof Floyd sold the diamonds. That's when I saw the vampire and five other men move through the barn carrying Remi's casket on their shoulders.

Raylene moved beside me. We fell in behind the pallbearers. Behind us the townspeople formed a long procession that started up the mountain with the sunset at our backs. Time runs differently on fairy land. I swear the sun stood still until we were all gathered around the open grave on the slope.

To my surprise, Aunt Saro Monroe moved forward to speak. Raylene leaned in and whispered against my ear, "She and Remi belonged to the same cooking group. The Barbgazi funeral rite requires a respected female elder to speak at the service."

Nodding, I turned my attention to the eulogy. Aunt Saro could be any age from fifty to a hundred. Dressed in black, but with a gaily patterned shawl wrapped around her thin shoulders, she spoke at length of Remi's love for good wine, food, the company of his friends, and the many quiet acts of kindness he performed in Miller's Cove.

"Remi kept his eyes turned to the hills," she said in closing. "He modeled the course of his life on their rise and fall, for in the depths of the windswept valley there always lies the hope of the sun-drenched summit. In the tradition of his kind, we now lay him to rest at the waning of the day so that his soul might rise with the dawn and climb to the eternal mountain to reside with his ancestors."

Using ropes, Press and the other pallbearers lowered the casket into the earth. Every mourner was asked to drop a rock into the grave before descending to the barn by the glow of the will-o'-the-wisps, who formed a long, solemn column of light in the deepening dusk.

I held back, planning to walk down the slope with Press so we'd have a chance to talk. While we waited, I heard rustling at the edge of the clearing. Straining my eyes to peer into the trees, I couldn't see anything in the shadows. I assumed a curious animal was watching us from the safety of deep cover, wondering at the way the two-foots carry on.

As I'd hoped, Press and I were the last at the grave. Punk and two of his brothers stood nearby waiting to finish the cairn when we left. I dropped my stone and sent Remi a heartfelt wish for a good climb. Reaching for Press's hand, we started to walk away.

Behind us the sound of claws scraping on stone stopped me. I heard Punk say, "What in tarnation is that?"

Fairy lights flared around us illuminating a small, purple creature standing atop the grave. White gauze covered one of its wings, which the being held tucked awkwardly against his side.

The grotesque face turned directly toward me. I assume that to the beast I looked like the least threatening humanoid in the clearing, the one that might believe the appeal that came next.

The hooked beak moved. In broken English, the imp said, "Remi-gazi good to Kryzdelt. Fixed hurt wing from chopping stick. Kryzdelt come to say good-bye to Remi-gazi. Not here to make trouble. Please believe, Kryzdelt. No hurt."

The voice sounded like fingernails on a chalkboard, but the words were clearing and the emotion behind them heartfelt. Everything fell into place for me like the pieces of Remi's jigsaw puzzle.

We were looking at an imp, the source of the purple stain on Frank's shoe, the victim of the hesitating strike of the hatchet, and the witness we needed to extract a double-murder confession from Floyd Reynolds.

Chapter 28

IMPS QUALIFY AS MINOR magical creatures. They've been portrayed in literature and art as crafty, even evil, but at most they're mischievous and easily influenced. An imp isn't capable of executing complicated plots on their own, but they're good at taking directions and serving as spies.

They love the spotlight, have a sense of humor on par with a hormonal teenage boy, and excel at irking humans. Physically the average imp stands less than a foot tall on all fours, their preferred means of getting around. Oversized ears flop down beside the twin horns that crown their bony heads.

Like all other minor paranormal beings, imps are banned in Miller's Cove because they're simply too hard to regulate and control. In the modern world, most function as gargoyles, spending their days frozen like stone on the facades of buildings, but free to roam at night.

Kryzdelt, the imp who now sat in the middle of the table in the barn's kitchen, had an unusually gregarious nature for his species. I cast a modulating spell to make listening to him less excruciating and retrieved a plate of food from the reception table, which he attacked with disgusting enthusiasm.

We'd brought Kryzdelt down from the burial site and hidden him in the kitchen rather than subject him to the scrutiny of the townspeople. Outside the door, the citizens of Miller's Cove spent the evening fulfilling the other aspect of a proper Barbgazi burial: celebrating the life of the deceased.

In the kitchen, we tried to bring Remi's killer to justice with the help of a purple, unpredictable prankster with a fractured and limited vocabulary. From the start, however, Kryzdelt communicated one message with total clarity—he loved Remi.

"Did Remi help you when you got hurt?" I asked the imp, trying to ignore the glob of tuna salad wedged in his beak.

Swallowing the over-sized bite with effort, Kryzdelt opened and closed his wings. The left didn't move as far as the right, thanks to both the wound and the bandage. "Chopping stick hurt Kryzdelt wing. Remi-gazi fix."

I looked at the clawed feet resting on the table. The middle toes of the back paws jutted well beyond the others, but all sported wicked, spiked claws—which explained the two puncture marks at the edge of Remi's desk.

Kryzdelt must have clutched at the wood with sufficient force to drill holes in the wood, probably while Remi treated the ax wound to the creature's wing.

It took most of the night to extract a coherent narrative from the imp, so I'll rearrange his story in chronological order. Kryzdelt and his coterie spent decades decorating the facade of an ostentatious mansion in Nashville.

When the city condemned the building following the death of the last family member, a wrecking crew demolished the structure. Fleeing for their lives, the imps fell under the influence of the Rabid Renegades, who saw nefarious potential in helping the impressionable creatures.

Over time, the Renegades refined the imps minimal shifting abilities, teaching them to change both form *and* size. Kryzdelt demonstrated for us by shrinking himself to the dimensions of my coffee cup and then morphing into an exact replica of the salt shaker on the table.

The Renegades cased the joint when Shawn took the busboy job at the Lodge. They identified the lack of modern technology and decided the imps would be perfect to capture credit card information by directly infiltrating guest's rooms.

Kryzdelt made the scratches on the dresser in Frank and Vanessa's quarters. The imp arrived disguised as one of the silver domes over the couple's room service order. Before they set the cart outside, the imp took refuge under one of the beds.

Frank turned, dimmed the lights and started his gangster movie marathon while Vanessa flipped through magazines and dozed on her side of the bed. When Kryzdelt emerged from hiding and prepared to make a move on Frank's wallet lying on the dresser, the imp spotted a small, velvet drawstring bag.

When he loosened the strings, Kryzdelt found the diamonds—at the exact moment Frank stood up to get ice. A series of bad choices by all concerned led to the ensuing events.

The imp panicked, scrambled for cover—scratching the dresser as he went—and knocked the room's ice bucket into the trash. He changed into a facsimile of the bucket, not realizing Frank would pick him up and carry him outside.

As an afterthought, Frank dropped the bag with the diamonds into his shirt pocket. At the ice machine, when he opened the door and leaned in to retrieve the scoop, the diamonds tumbled out of his pocket.

Swearing, Frank put the ice bucket/imp down and knelt to search for the gemstones. Kryzdelt shifted back to his native form, but several sizes smaller than normal. He perched on Frank's neck to get a good view of what was going on in the ice machine.

Thinking a bug landed on his neck, Frank took a swipe at the imp. Kryzdelt made a grab to steady himself, scratching Frank in the process. That's when Floyd came out of the darkness armed with a hatchet.

The imp tried to take flight, but Floyd delivered a savage blow that clipped the creature's wing. Crying in pain, Kryzdelt fled into the shadows. When he looked back, he saw the "chopping stick" embedded in Frank's skull while Floyd leaned over the body and into the ice machine.

Imps have thick, gelatinous blood. Kryzdelt saw the stain on Frank's shoe. Normally, as the Renegades had taught him to do, the imp would have gone back and tried to cover his tracks—even to the point of mopping up his own blood.

In this case, with Floyd still on the scene, the imp couldn't take those precautions. Instead, he watched the human who hurt him remove the scoop from the machine and walk away. The velvet bag rested atop the ice Floyd retrieved.

Later that night, Remi found the injured imp cowering in a storage room down the hall from the Barbgazi's office. At this point in his story, Kryzdelt made a mournful noise.

"Remi-gazi carry Kryzdelt to safe room. Put sticky goop and white stuff on wing. Kryzdelt slept in Remi-gazi cave. Helped with broken picture."

Translation: Remi took the wounded imp home, cared for him, and taught the creature how to work a jigsaw puzzle.

"Remi-gazi ask why Kryzdelt there," the imp said. "Kryzdelt said truth. Remi-gazi talk with wolf-boy about plastic numbers. Said taking plastic bad, but wanted wolf boy and Kryzdelt friends be safe."

Later, a conversation with Shawn (and some details picked up from Floyd) helped us decipher the more vague points of the imp's story.

Already suspicious after speaking with the credit card companies about the fake charges, Remi got the whole story out of Shawn—including the details of the gang's blackmailing the boy by threatening his sister.

Remi also knew that imps were banned in Miller's Cove. Fearing that the creatures might be punished, the Barbgazi wanted to ensure their safety before telling the authorities what had been going on at the Lodge.

That was the assurance he hoped to gain from Press. Before I could convey the request to the vampire in a private setting, Floyd Reynolds struck again.

When he and Vanessa entered the lobby the night we saw them from the ice machine, they wanted to settle their bill with the lodge for a planned dawn departure. Apparently over dinner and drinks at the Copycat, the duo decided to get out of town fast.

They found the front desk deserted. Floyd sent Vanessa to her room to pack while he tried to locate someone on staff. He found his way into the lower maze of offices and followed the light to where Remi sat talking with the imp.

Floyd must have lingered outside the door long enough to hear the creature provide an even more detailed account of Frank's death. When the imp said that the "man with the chopping stick" looked just like "the man with the shiny rocks," Floyd panicked.

He snatched the fire ax off the wall and killed Remi first to make sure the Barbgazi couldn't tell anyone what he'd heard. Floyd came after Kryzdelt next, but he underestimated the imp's powers. When Floyd looked at the desk, he saw nothing but papers and a bottle of red wine.

Assuming the shape of that bottle saved the imp's life. When Floyd left, Kryzdelt went to Remi, stroking his hand, hoping to wake him up and leaving the faint scratches I'd detected. When the imp heard the custodian's cart in the hall, Kryzdelt hid among the objets d'art on the shelf where he remained throughout the day—even while we were in the room questioning Shawn.

Using that stealthy advantage, the imp learned about Remi's funeral and contrived to stowaway in Press's car so he could attend the service. That's how he came to be on the mountainside, where we found him at the Barbgazi's grave.

If you're thinking that Press would have a hard time pinning a double murder on Floyd Reynolds based on the testimony of an imp, you're right. But don't forget that the vampire arranged a final night of bonding for the Reynolds twins that led to a phone call from the station in the wee hours of the morning.

Punk came into the kitchen and told Press about the change of heart Floyd Reynolds experienced after some time alone in his jail cell. He wanted to see the Chief of Police immediately. Far from demanding legal counsel, Floyd wanted to talk.

Before Press granted that wish, however, he drove Buckshot home. Standing in his dark driveway, the mayor put his hands on the roof of the Plymouth and looked down at Press. "I'm going to bed. When I wake up, I want to hear that you have an iron-clad case against Floyd Reynolds that does not include a single mention of imps."

"Roger that," Press said. "Confession minus imps. Not a problem."

As we drove away, I looked at the vampire's profile in the dim light. "How are you planning on getting Floyd to expunge little purple gargoyles from his story?"

"By having Jerry hum him a sweet tune. Trust me."

Press dropped me at the house. When he walked me to the door, the vampire said, "Get some sleep and meet me at the Deja Vu for breakfast at 8. I think this will all be wrapped up by then."

Yeah, I wanted to go with him to the station, but putting the squeeze to Floyd was Press's job, not mine. My part of the case required a different kind of final act.

"Make it 8:30," I said, standing on tiptoe and aiming a kiss at the vampire's cheek. So much for best laid plans. Press turned his head so that our lips met in a feather-light touch that was, for me, the perfect mix of fire and ice.

"See you then," he whispered against my mouth before striding confidently into the darkness.

From the other end of the porch, the ghost of Frank Reynolds materialized. "You two make a really good pair. I remember what happened now."

Normally, I don't drop the wards on my house for spirits. That's a level of taking my work home with which I don't choose to deal, but Frank had grown on me.

Unlocking the door, physically and magically, I said, "Come on in, Frank. We have a few things to discuss."

Unfortunately, my paycheck wouldn't be part of that conversation. I'd already given up on getting paid, but there's more to that story, too. Keep reading.

Chapter 29

FRANK FLOATED INTO the foyer and hovered by the door to the den. When I invited him to have a seat, he said, "This isn't the room where you like to be. There's barely any trace of your energy here. It would be nicer for you if we talked in the study."

"When did you get so stable and coherent?" I asked. "*Hey!* Where's the hatchet?"

The ghost actually twirled to show me his new blade-free status. "You have no idea how good it feels to have that thing out of my head. I started clearing up in the jail cell with my brother. When he broke and started begging to speak to your friend, Chief Jackson, the hatchet disappeared and I was me again. Really, a *better* version of me."

I never like to hear someone say they had to die to embrace self-improvement, but I've heard other spirits say similar things. "You can see everything in a different light now, can't you?"

We'd gone into the study, and I lit the electric logs. Frank sat across from me by the hearth. He was completely relaxed, with his legs crossed and hands resting in his lap. The poor guy looked so lifelike, I briefly considered offering him a drink.

"Yes, I see it all now. Vanessa married me for my money, and we had none of the same interests. She isn't a bad woman, but she grew up desperately poor. Her looks are her only skill, so men are an effective investment strategy for her."

"But she had you," I said, "and you were happy in the marriage. I've seen the receipts. You didn't curtail her spending at all. Why would she have an affair with your brother?"

Frank shrugged. "Because Floyd is a no good louse who made it his life mission to take everything from me, and Vanessa fell for his lies?"

Yeah. That explanation worked. "So what did you do to brother dearest last night?"

"Took him for a ride down memory lane," the ghost said, laughing. "I offered to repeat the journey every night for the rest of his life. Our grandfather read *A Christmas Carol* to us when we were kids. The story scared the hell out of my brother. He didn't want to live stuck in *that* plot to the end of his days."

"But Scrooge reformed himself in the end."

"Frank never got to that part of the story. He didn't even make it to the Ghost of Christmas Future before he ran out of the room crying. I may have given the book an alternate ending when I discussed it with him last night."

After a beat, we both burst out laughing. "Good for you," I said. "Your brother belongs in the Jerk Hall of Fame."

"You have no idea. There's one thing I truly regret about this mess, however, and I don't know how to make it right."

I had a pretty good idea how he would answer. The diamonds Frank planned to sell to Mandrake carried a rough value of $150,000, but by accepting the discontinued paper money, Frank could have raked in as much as $450,000.

"The numismatic value of the currency depended on condition," he explained, "but from what I could tell watching Floyd, the bills would command top dollar. I shouldn't have done that to Mandrake."

Trying to skirt the author's identity as a dragon shifter, I said, "He wanted the diamonds more than the paper money."

"What you said about the view being different on my side?" Frank said. "Well, I know what you all are. The idea that Miller's Cove could transport me back in time appealed to me when Vanessas and I came here, but I wish I'd known magical creatures lived in town."

"It's not something we can put in the Chamber of Commerce literature."

"Yeah, I get that," he said, "but you're all wonderful people. I appreciate the way you've helped me. Do you think you can see that Mandrake gets to keep the diamonds and his money?"

I was starting to wish I'd known the living Frank Reynolds. "But what about Vanessa?"

"She'll be getting a nice inheritance. I'm happy for her to have my money so long as she's not sharing it with Floyd."

As diplomatically as I could make the point, I said, "You know she'll probably find another husband. You said so yourself in the car that first day."

The ghost sighed. "I think you can understand that having just been murdered, I wasn't at my best. Vanessa can do whatever she likes with her life. That's the *privilege* of being alive."

"What are you going to do?"

"Go out to the Nostalgia Nook and stay with Vanessa until dawn. Then I'm going to take a walk into the rising sun."

With his path revealed to him, Frank had embraced the need to move on to whatever came next.

When I yawned, he said, "Please don't let me keep you up. I just wanted to thank you for everything and to say I'm sorry you won't be paid."

I made a dismissive gesture. "Don't worry about it. This case came with a different set of rewards."

The ghost stood and moved toward the door. Before he left me for the last time, Frank said, "When you dress for your breakfast with Chief Jackson, put your hair up in those..." He made vague circular gestures over his forehead.

Smothering a smile, I said, "Victory rolls. They're called victory rolls."

"Yeah, do that. Chief Jackson likes your hair that way. Oh, and tell Raylene I'm sorry I never got to taste her pimento cheese. It looks to die for."

With that, Frank Reynolds passed through the closed door to the kitchen and out of my life. I don't miss all of my clients, but I'll miss him.

After catching three or four hours of sleep, I did what Frank suggested and carefully arranged my hair in thick victory rolls. Choosing a crisp poplin blouse in soft lavender and gray slacks with deep pleats, I surveyed myself in the standing mirror. Not bad for a gal functioning on two nights of almost no sleep.

On the way to meet Press at the Deja Vu, I stopped by and picked up Raylene. She deserved to hear the case wrap-up in person. Already dressed for work in one of her smart, belted suits, my best friend looked well rested and refreshed.

"What time did you get to bed?" she asked, climbing into the Dodge and giving me a hug.

"I honestly can't tell you. Frank Reynolds came over for a late night talk."

On the way to the diner, I caught her up on the Kryzdelt story. We found Press already seated in our booth, information Rosie passed on when we came in the front door with a knowing wink.

The vampire stood as we approached the table. "Good morning, ladies. You both look beautiful this gorgeous Monday morning."

Press Jackson never calls any morning gorgeous. "You're in a good mood," I said, sliding onto the bench seat with Raylene beside me. "Things went well with Floyd?"

"Oh," the vampire grinned. "I'd say things went very well."

When Press and Jerry put Floyd in an interrogation room around 4 a.m. the suspect couldn't wait to spill everything. He admitted to the affair with Vanessa and the plan to take the diamonds from his brother.

Floyd drove his own car from St. Louis to Miller's Cove. He arrived at the Nostalgia Nook in time to watch his brother kneel at the ice machine—with a "hideous purple monster" on his neck.

As unbelievable as I found the revelation, Floyd really did enjoy camping. He had the hatchet in his trunk and claimed to have grabbed the weapon to "kill that thing attacking Frank."

None of us at the table bought that part of the story. Going after an imp—who was, at the time, no larger than a man's fist—with a hatchet defined "overkill." Regardless of the target, Floyd did manage to both wound Kryzdelt and kill Frank.

"He says he didn't mean to knock off his brother," Press said, biting into a crunchy piece of bacon, "and even with the diamond angle, proving premeditated murder will be hard, but manslaughter's a slam dunk."

For an "accidental" killer, Floyd showed remarkable presence of mind that night. He used the ice scoop to retrieve the diamonds, not realizing until later that one had been lost inside the machine.

Undaunted, he concluded the deal with Mandrake. "Poor sap admits he and the dame should have left town then," Press said, "but Vanessa had her heart set on a night at the Copycat looking like Ingrid Bergman."

The actress she couldn't have identified in a line-up to save her life.

That desire on Vanessa's part put Floyd on a collision course with actual murder in the first degree. He confessed to killing Remi when he realized the Barbgazi knew the truth of Frank's death.

"Jerry's going over Floyd's statement with him now," Press said, "and using his siren skills to keep the facts intact without any mention of little purple monsters. Jerry will hum his way through a talk with Vanessa, too, to make certain she doesn't say anything that will implicate the imp."

"So," Raylene said, "the diamonds were legal, the first murder may have been an accident, the credit card fraud involved blackmailing an innocent, Mandrake willingly parted with the $500 bills, Remi's death was premeditated murder, and we have imps in Miller's Cove."

She ticked off each of the points with a flick of a well-manicured nail, then looked to Press for confirmation.

"That about sums it up," the vampire said, "but I can add two details. Buckshot plans to locate Susie Pruitt and try to adopt both kids. They'll be better off living here among their own kind. As for the imps, the Joneses have agreed to take them in. The will-o'-the-wisps can keep the creatures corralled to the boundaries of the property."

I'll admit that breakfast felt somewhat anticlimactic after the whirlwind investigation of the last three days, but I did find the resolution of Frank Reynolds's death satisfying. Not from the justice angle, but for the image of the victim himself walking happily into the rays of the rising sun.

Raylene and I made plans to take Aqua Netta to the picture show that evening since Mondays at the Memory Palace are never busy. Even in Miller's Cove, propping a talking vase up on a theater seat could get a person some strange looks.

To our surprise, Press asked to come along and we agreed. I left the Deja Vu feeling like my social life had taken a positive turn, even if my finances weren't so lucky.

Going in the far end of the alley, I dropped Raylene at Bygone Beauty and parked beside Uncle Grim's Model A. When I got out of the car, I doused myself with barrier magic and went into the shop.

Like any other day at Tucker's Horology, I found Grim at his workbench. "Morning," he said. "Understand your case got all wrapped up."

The gossip rocket strikes again. "It did," I said, "but this one's going in the books as a loss, money wise."

"Oh," Grim said, "I don't know so much about that. Here."

He pushed an envelope in my direction. When I opened the flap, I found three mint condition $500 bills inside. "What's this?"

"Mandrake said he heard a voice that sounded like Frank's in a dream last night saying you should be paid," Grim explained. "Manny doesn't care about the paper money. He said to say thanks because he's incorporating an ax murder in his new book."

When the bell on the front door dinged, I dropped the bills in my bag and headed out to play proper clock shop lady. Two men died, but two children were well on their way to rescue and the imps would be safe and free—and even if it was a foursome, I had a sort of date with Press.

Not a bad way to start a new week in Miller's Cove.

A Note from the Author

Hi! Thank you for reading *Axed at the Ice Machine*. You may have noticed on the cover that the author of this book appears as "Rana K. Williamson writing as Juliette Harper."

The Mattie Tucker books are a "bridge" series from my prior writing partnership to producing books as a solo author.

I have many exciting projects in development. To sign up for my email list, please visit my website at www.ranakwilliamson.com and click "Subscribe" in the upper right.

You can also connect with me on Facebook from the site. I run a private readers' group there, which I invite you to join.

I'm also pleased to announce that I'm hosting *The Journals of Jym Ann Adair* on Patreon as well as providing exclusive benefits to my subscribers involving everything I'm writing.

Jym Ann is a paranormal agent with the shadowy (and fictional) LDT Division of the Texas Rangers. As she puts it, LDT agents aren't devils, but they do hunt them. New episodes appear each Friday, with no end in sight!

Click the link on my website or go directly to www.patreon.com/ranakwilliamson

And just turn the page for a sneak peek of *Corpse on the Set*, the second Mattie Tucker mystery, currently available on Amazon!

Sneak Peek of *Corpse on the Set*

The woman stood in the middle of the pink tiled bathroom, arms folded over her chest. Carefully coiffed blonde curls tumbled over the shoulders of her terrycloth bathrobe. The scene made for a pretty picture until she started talking. "I'm sorry. Tell me your name again."

"Mattie Tucker."

"Well, Mattie Tucker. I want *my* electric toothbrush."

Living in Miller's Cove, the South's premier nostalgia destination, demands being a good student of history. We hold to a mix of 1930s/1940s ambiance, which explains why super star actress Natalie Evander was arguing with me that late summer morning.

Boy-genius director Allen Stillwater sent the entire cast of his planned remake of the 1946 classic *The Best Years of Our Lives* to our town to "immerse themselves in the war-time milieu."

When I read the article from the local paper to my Uncle Grim, he was working on a mantel clock in the backroom of our business, Tucker's Horology.

Peering into the clock's guts through his magnifying loupe, Grim said, "What does mildew have to do with World War II?"

"*Milieu*, not mildew. It's a fancy word for social environment."

As I continued to scan the article, I came to the part that ultimately would land me in hot water: "period lifestyle coaches wanted."

The clock shop turns a good profit, more from Grim's expert repairs than outright sales, and I work as a paranormal private investigator.

For me to earn money, however, an unhappy ghost has to show up on my doorstep requesting help—preferably with a link to a living person in possession of a healthy bank account.

The dead had been resting too well for my profit margin for a couple of months. I could use the cash, and how hard could it be to teach someone how to live in the past?

I hadn't met Natalie Evander yet.

To be truthful, I didn't even know the woman's work. Our local theater, the Majestic Memory Palace, only shows films from Hollywood's Golden Age.

When I learned Stillwater cast Ms. Evander in the Myrna Loy role from the original film, I expected someone like Myrna Loy.

Known as The Queen of Hollywood in the 1930s, Loy ranked as one of the most beloved actresses of her time. Talented and beautiful, she also kept her personal dramas private.

Now I had a cranky starlet camped out in a rented house across the street from my gracious old Craftsman. I thought having Natalie so close to my house would facilitate our lessons. I didn't know it would have me running back and forth across the street putting up with tantrums.

The actress not only wanted her electric toothbrush, she wanted her social media and the constant diet of adoring attention it supplied.

As for the toothbrush, I ran down a period-correct model that looked more like a power tool than a dental hygiene device. When I presented it to Natalie, she recoiled in horror.

Embracing my role as an educator, I tried to explain that electric toothbrushes didn't come into widespread use until 1960. In response, I found myself confronted by the full-range of the celebrity's logic-based debate skills.

"So?"

"So, Mr. Stillwater wants you to live a strictly 1940s lifestyle while you're in Miller's Cove. Specifically, the war years, 1941 to 1945."

Myrna Loy starred in *The Best Years of Our Lives* at the age of 41. Natalie Evander would turn 25 in a week. How much difference can 16 years make, you ask? Judge for yourself based on what the actress said next.

"You're stifling my creative potential and making my aura spark. I'm going to tell my agent."

Did I mention Natalie's mother also serves as her agent? Me and my bright ideas about making easy money.

About the Author

Hi! Thank you for reading *Axed at the Ice Machine*. You may have noticed on the cover that the author of this book appears as "Rana K. Williamson writing as Juliette Harper."

The Mattie Tucker books are a "bridge" series from my prior writing partnership to producing books as a solo author.

I have many exciting projects in development. To sign up for my email list, please visit my website at www.ranakwilliamson.com and click "Subscribe" in the upper right.

You can also connect with me on Facebook from the site. I run a private readers' group there, which I invite you to join.

I'm also pleased to announce that I'm hosting *The Journals of Jym Ann Adair* on Patreon as well as providing exclusive benefits to my subscribers involving everything I'm writing.

Jym Ann is a paranormal agent with the shadowy (and fictional) LDT Division of the Texas Rangers. As she puts it, LDT agents aren't devils, but they do hunt them. New episodes appear each Friday, with no end in sight!

Click the link on my website or go directly to www.patreon.com/ranakwilliamson

Read more at www.ranakwilliamson.com.

www.ingramcontent.com/pod-product-compliance
Lightning Source LLC
Chambersburg PA
CBHW051502170626
46811CB00002B/609